ZACH KRYTON
THRILLER

GUARDRAIL

JOSH
FRANCIS

Guardrail – A Zach Kryton Thriller (Book 5)

This is the second book in the storyline that continues chronologically after the <u>Zach Kryton Introductory Series</u> – it is recommended you read this series first.

WARNING: some obscene language

Josh Francis

ISBN: 978-0-6487025-4-2 (paperback)

Published by Red Diamond independent publishing

Josh is seeking formal representation for his works

www.red-diamond.com.au/books

<u>Sign up to the reader's group</u>

This story is fictional!

Cover media by Onur Aksoy – Great work Onur!
www.onegraphica.com

Also By Josh Francis

Pegasus – The Zach Kryton Introductory Series (Book 1).

Poseidon – The Zach Kryton Introductory Series (Book 2).

Phoenix – The Zach Kryton Introductory Series (Book 3).

Greyfin – A Zach Kryton Thriller (Book 4).

Battle Rhythm – The military-inspired personal planning, discipline and motivation guide (The Camouflage Series Book 1).

Centre of Gravity – The principles soldiers use to think, act and achieve success (The Camouflage Series Book 2).

Under the Pump – Anecdotes of a service station operator (E-Book).

Follow Us

You can find other publications and join our conversations on social media. This will keep you up to date with upcoming books and allow you to share ideas. Feel free to contribute!

INSTAGRAM

FACEBOOK

AMAZON

Please leave an honest review on Amazon. This helps to tailor and improve the content of what we produce.

Contents

1

The faint wailing noise echoed across the early morning air as Zach Kryton stood outside looking over the desert sky. The haunting sound emanating over numerous loudspeakers, conducted by the local Imam, indicated that sunrise was imminent, and the faithful would soon undertake the Fajr prayers.

Kryton usually cherished viewing the majestic purple that filled the sky during the morning twilight as the night slowly transitioned into a new day. However, he could have just as easily been looking at a brick wall for all the attention he was actually paying to it.

His mind continued to race.

Less than eight hours earlier, his Greyfin team had been in Dubai, about to capture the main suspect in the killing of a former Russian nuclear scientist on Australian shores. A scientist placed in hiding by the U.S. after he had defected from the motherland, bringing his knowledge of nuclear secrets with him.

That scientist was now dead, and U.S. and Australian intelligence authorities were still scrambling to find out how his closely guarded hiding location had been discovered.

Their only lead: the man they were referring to as 'Boyd'. This was based on the suspect's fraudulent use of a passport belonging to a long dead Australian tourist. The Greyfin analysts in Canberra had tracked Boyd across South-East Asia and into the Middle East, where his trail was picked up by an Australian Army surveillance team.

Just as they were about to make a discreet interception, the Greyfin field team was disrupted by a team of armed bandits who had spooked Boyd, who made a hasty escape, but not before injuring one of the young Aussie soldiers.

Two of those bandits were now sitting inside the isolated, disused warehouse in the middle of the Dubai desert that Kryton stood next to, being closely guarded by a small team of close protection experts from the Royal Australian Air Force's Airfield Defence Guards. Affectionately known as Adgies, these airmen were on deployment to the Australian forward compound at the Al-Minhad Air Base, and were the best military asset that could be mustered at short notice.

Kryton inhaled deeply. The air had already started turning a dry warm, and another hot day was to be expected. His thought process was disrupted by the crunching of sand under shoes close to him. He turned his head to see Cav join him, also looking out to the morning sky.

Cav stifled a yawn.

"Get any sleep?" asked Kryton.

Cav just shook his head.

"Nah…I think I passed the point of tired a few hours back. I'm in that foggy but awake zone now."

Kryton nodded as he returned his gaze across the desert. He knew what Cav meant. Despite how they were portrayed in the movies, special operations were typically long hours of boredom interwoven with brief periods of intense action. Those working in that world had to quickly become used to operating at high levels for long hours on little to no sleep. The Greyfin team had experienced all of that in the past two days.

"So, what now?" asked Cav.

"Well, let's recap what we've got here. Two POIs inside who are well trained and not saying anything, and, if Jonas is right, are both Mossad agents; a dead nuclear scientist killed on our turf, with possibly more now vulnerable to being compromised in their supposedly secret hiding places; and, the only suspect to all this mayhem has escaped after injuring a digger…"

"Who's going just fine. Clay went with him back to AMAB to ensure he gets patched up," interjected Cav, reassuring Kryton, who was still blaming himself for a casualty that occurred during the mission he was in command of.

"Who's going to be fine," repeated Kryton, "but no thanks to the man whose whereabouts are currently unknown."

"Sounds about right," agreed Cav.

Kryton chuckled.

Hell of a week, he thought to himself.

At that moment, Jo joined the two men, looking just as tired as they both felt. She passed an encrypted satellite phone to Kryton.

"It's Jonas," she said quietly.

"Yes, mate?" Kryton said, stepping away from the side of the warehouse where the dull noise of a transmitter providing irregular electricity would make it hard to hear the Australian spy back in Canberra.

"What's the situation?" Jonas asked.

"No change," Kryton replied. "They're obviously well briefed and trained. They haven't said anything apart from claiming their innocence and stating that they're private security for some Sheik."

Back in the Greyfin operations room, Jonas could only smile.

"I guess once they realised that we weren't going to put the screws to them, they felt comfortable in closing ranks."

"Yeah. We've given them some water and food that the Adgies brought out, and provided medical attention. I think they realise that we're not going to harm them, but they're still playing the game and sticking to the book regardless. Anyway, how long till their boss gets here?" asked Kryton.

After detaining the two bandits after a brief but violent fight in the dusty loading area of the Dubai Mall, their photographs were run through the various systems of the five-eyes intelligence community.

Those systems had long memories, and some very powerful facial recognition software. If a young tourist had been to America, or any of the other anglophone nations that shared their intelligence, then their image would become a permanent presence in the systems from when they had passed through the visa check at the border. Should that same person's image pop up again later on – say as an intelligence agent trying to utilise a different name to conduct covert work in a five-eyes nation – then their true identity might be established more easily, and more details could be added to their individual files over time.

It had quickly been established that the two individuals now in Greyfin's custody were, in fact, known Mossad agents.

Their mission? They weren't saying. But it had led to some rapid and highly confidential diplomatic calls through various embassies and intelligence agencies, and the CIA had ultimately alerted their Mossad contacts that two of their agents were sitting in an old, but still useable, CIA safehouse outside Dubai.

"He's on his way now from Cairo. His name is Jacob Levy, and he's a registered diplomatic officer. He'll be bringing his assistant with him, but we don't know who that will be. CIA were happy to provide your location, so they will be coming to you."

"What's the catch?" asked Kryton, sensing an issue with the plan.

"Well, Levy is Mossad for sure. CIA had him on the list of official contacts. Which means that they're probably field agents, but using diplomatic cover. The Israelis tried to deny their actual identity at first, obviously, but once we showed them our evidence of their previous ops, they admitted that they were theirs, and now they are demanding them back."

"Did they say what they were doing in a Dubai pub armed with weapons?" asked Kryton.

Jonas scoffed.

"Yeah, of course they did – in great detail," he replied sarcastically.

Kryton rolled his eyes upon realising the ignorance of the question. He was more tired than he thought.

"That is what *you* need to try and find out," said Jonas, in a more serious tone.

Kryton rubbed his hand over his face, looking out over the desert as the sun commenced its ascent into the now orange sky. The two Australians quickly discussed some of the admin details of the handover.

"Jonas, did we fuck up?"

"No, mate. We've reviewed your report; the movements of the blue force; as well as the radio comms. It looks like it's just pure arse that you've been interrupted by these people. Unfortunate, too. We've got every alert imaginable out. If Boyd pops up again, we'll find him."

Kryton breathed a sigh of relief. He quietly believed they had not been reckless during the surveillance operation, but years of experience taught him that intelligence failures often required someone – usually at the bottom – to take the blame.

"Okay. What now?"

"Speak to Levy." said Jonas. "Apologise profusely to show him some love; but don't take responsibility, and ensure you protect our own mission. We're guessing that we simply interrupted a standard low-level field operation. Let's face it, the Israelis carry weapons in the Middle East as a matter of practice. But…"

"But, what?" asked Kryton.

4

"But don't assume anything or trust them. These two might not be deep cover, but they were still doing something that they will now have to assume is compromised, even if we don't actually know what it was."

Kryton sighed.

"Roger. Love playing spy games," he lamented as he terminated the call to Australia.

He returned to the side of the warehouse where Cav and Jo were sitting against the wall, resting for a moment. He kneeled down next to them.

"Well, good news is, it looks like we were just in the wrong place at the wrong time."

"Or they were," stated Jo, with her still eyes closed.

"Or that," said Kryton. "Anyway, we're not being blamed."

"And the bad news?" asked Cav, knowing that there are always two sides to a coin.

"Well, someone from the Israeli mission is inbound to collect these two, so I have to deal with that first. However, that should be the end of this part of the saga."

"And then?" asked Jo.

Kryton just shrugged his shoulders.

"Then, we wait for further instructions. Boyd has disappeared back into the ether. He might as well be a ghost at this point."

Cav and Jo just looked at each other. They were as frustrated as Kryton. They wanted the mission to have been as successful as much as he did, but right now it felt like a complete failure. They had literally been on top of Boyd. But, as the old adage says, miss by and inch, miss by a mile.

He smiled as he stood up.

"I'll go check on our guests. We'll probably be here for a while yet, and it'll be bloody warm today. Find some shade and get some rest."

In no time at all, both Cav and Jo fell fast asleep tucked up against the wheel-well of their white 4WD vehicle.

It was far too hot to try to sleep inside the warehouse.

Kryton peered inside through the door at the two Mossad agents sitting upright at a table in the middle of the barren building. Their hands were still bound, but they had movement of their arms so they could access the water bottles sitting in front of them. He nodded to the young, plain clothes Adgie standing guard by the door as he entered, before proceeding to walk over to where the man and woman both sat.

5

He looked down at them.

"Your boss will be here soon. Once we're happy all is okay, you'll be handed over. Do you need anything?"

The woman looked like she was about to say something, but a sharp glance from her colleague forced her to pause. Their faces were injured from their respective encounters with Cav and Jo, and the bruises were now ripening. Kryton felt a little sorry for them – but not too much. Whoever they were, and whatever they were doing, these two had disrupted his mission. He decided to leave them be.

"Make sure they get regular bathroom use. Don't let them out of your sight for a moment," said Kryton to the head of the Adgie detachment as he left the warehouse.

"Yes, sir," came the disciplined reply.

He moved over to join his teammates by 4WD. He knew he could trust the airmen to maintain watch. In a few minutes, he was fast asleep himself.

2

The warm air still permeated throughout the night as Kryton and his team awaited the arrival of the Israeli diplomat. They had made the most of the hours of waiting by catching up on sleep and discussing options to continue the mission after the handover of the two detained bandits had occurred. As a result, they were all now highly alert, and keen to get on with the job.

Kryton fiddled with his ear, adjusting the small wire which was linked to the earpiece that connected his radio to the satellite phone, which held the connection back to HQ.

"Shouldn't be long now?" he asked Jonas across his concealed mic.

"Inbound, about five minutes out. We're tracking a single black SUV. Three occupants. Definitely Levy in the front passenger's seat. A female in the rear behind him, and what looks like a local driver," replied Jonas, looking at the clear video feed from the Predator that was circling nearly four miles above them.

The perfectly clear evening provided just enough ambient light to make for quality viewing.

Kryton looked to the sky as he acknowledged the brief from Jonas, and then ensured that the rest of the team was aware. The Predator was hiding in the darkness. Kryton smiled; just knowing it was there always provided him a sense of comfort and tactical advantage.

"The CIA sure picked a good spot for this place. We can see all the approaches," said Cav as he moved next to Kryton.

Kryton nodded in agreement. Although in all reality this should be a fairly smooth and amicable process, he didn't want to leave anything to chance.

"Where did you put the marksman?" he asked Cav.

Cav turned and pointed up in the direction of the only road leading to the warehouse.

"About 200 metres up and in a small bit of dead ground. The Adgies have a cutoff set up in their 4WD."

"Good. I doubt we'll need it," said Kryton. "The Adgies aren't trigger happy, I hope."

Cav chuckled.

"Nah, they're good. Their team leader is on the long gun. He's a qualified combat controller," he said, referring to the special forces trained element of the RAAF.

Jo was the first to spot the dim beam of the approaching headlights.

"Here we go," she said from her position by the front of the warehouse a few feet from her counterparts.

"Jonas, we spot headlights to our east."

"That's your guests," replied Jonas across the satellite phone.

The faint lights grew even brighter as the vehicle rapidly approached, occasionally appearing to bounce as it transited over the undulating terrain of the road.

"Shit; they're cruising," observed Cav.

Both he and Kryton instinctively placed their hands over their concealed weapons. In less than a minute, the SUV came to a sudden halt less than twenty metres from the warehouse. The Australians had to shield their eyes from high beams.

Kryton waved his hand to instruct the driver to lower the intensity of the headlights. It had an instantaneous effect, and the lights suddenly dimmed to a more palatable wattage.

For a few moments, there was no movement. The three Australians just looked at the motionless SUV with its engine still running. Kryton looked at Cav, who returned the gaze with a slight shrug of his shoulders.

Although the three of them felt the more vulnerable of the two sides, in reality it was the occupants of the SUV, who unknowingly had professionally trained weapons pointed at them from the shadows on multiple sides.

Kryton placed his arms deliberately by his side and turned his palms outwards, moving diagonally away from the front of the vehicle and out of the spotlight. He could now see the silhouettes of three people, exactly in the locations as described by Jonas.

A few seconds later, the two doors on the right-hand side of the SUV opened. Kryton's eyes soon adjusted as he moved away from the lights, and he could see both a male and a female step out and slowly walk towards him.

They both stopped a few feet in front of him. The female was about Jo's age and height, wearing a dark skirt with matching coat, with her curly dark hair tightly tied up in a pony tail.

The male was something out of a 70s political-spy movie. Of thin build and just over six-feet in height, wearing a crumpled beige suit jacket over dark pants, with a loosened thick striped tie, Kryton guessed him to be in his late 50's. It was the thick, dark framed glasses that almost made Kryton laugh.

The man stepped forward, smiling and extending a large hand.

"My name is Jacob Levy. I am the First Political Secretary from the Cairo Embassy of the state of Israel."

Kryton also took a pace forward, taking Levy's hand and greeting him in turn.

"I'm Zach. Australian Army. Nice to meet you, sir," said Kryton, deliberately leaving out his surname.

He looked closely at the man in front of him. His clothes and words might have said diplomat, but his firm handshake and the intensity of his eyes screamed spy.

"This is my deputy, Miss Gadot," said Levy, motioning to the well-dressed assistant.

Kryton nodded at her in acknowledgement, before quickly returning his attention to Levy.

"I'm sure you'd like to see your people. Would you please come this way. My colleagues will look after your assistant."

Levy nodded, following Kryton into the warehouse.

They walked over to the table where the two Israeli agents sat. Upon seeing Levy, they both stood up obediently – an instinctive action in military units globally upon seeing a superior. It simply confirmed to Kryton that Levy was not just a mere diplomat.

Levy said a few indistinguishable words to his people. Kryton assumed it to be Yiddish or Hebrew. The tired Mossad agents engaged in a quick conversation with their boss. The older man smiled and placed his hand reassuringly on the female's shoulder, before turning his attention back to Kryton.

"Surely we can remove these?" he said, motioning to the flexicuffs that were restraining the agent's hands.

Kryton thought for a moment, then nodded. He motioned at the young Adgie, who moved over to remove the restraints. Although they had deliberately been left somewhat loose, the two detainees rubbed their wrists in relief, stretching their shoulders and trying to get their body to return to a more natural feeling.

"Bring in some more water," Kryton said into his radio.

Cav dutifully obeyed, bringing in some fresh bottles which were well received by the two agents who had spent the majority of the day inside a stifling air-condition-less building. Kryton made a point of not introducing the commando to Levy, instead guiding the Israeli back out into the evening night.

Kryton was about to talk, but was cut off immediately by Levy, whose initial friendly demeanour suddenly took a more assertive tone.

"I demand that my people be released into my custody immediately," he said, pulling two pieces of paper from his jacket pocket and handing them to Kryton.

"We'll get to that in a moment," retorted Kryton, taking the documents and tilting them slightly to shine some light from the dim glow of the external lighting of the warehouse onto them.

He examined them closely. The first document had clear images of the two agents – a copy of their diplomatic passports, with their names redacted. The second was ostensibly a letter from the UAE government directing the two 'diplomats' be released.

They were clearly fakes. The Israelis wouldn't dare inform the Arabic host nation of their presence. Kryton didn't know whether to laugh or feel insulted. It didn't matter. His direction was to get any information from Levy as to what had occurred; to assess if their own mission had been compromised; and, to then get rid of the agents from his custody.

The U.S. had decided it wanted nothing to do with the Mossad right now, and the Australians were inclined to agree.

"Your agents – your *Mossad* agents – interrupted a host nation approved military counter-terrorism operation we were running. They then attacked my people, whilst armed. Why?" asked Kryton calmly.

Levy paused for a moment. Kryton could see his mind processing Kryton's question, which indicated that he hadn't known that the Australians knew who they really were. Like the seasoned operator that he obviously was, though, Levy was ready with a viable answer, feeling no need to keep up pretences. He smiled at Kryton. A smile of respect that suggested he knew that his counterpart was also a seasoned operator.

"Yes, and for that I apologise. We appreciate your candour regarding the status of our agents. We were also running a training exercise. The two people inside there are trainees. Their personal details of which I cannot enter into. I'm sure you understand," said Levy.

Kryton looked back down at the documents, ostensibly re-reading them, but in actuality making an assessment of the situation.

"And their weapons?" Kryton asked, already knowing the answer to the question, but wanting to see how Levy would answer it.

The Israeli's patter was flawless.

"As you can imagine, it's hard for us Jews to operate in this part of the world. This environment is invaluable for training before our agents move into…the more difficult parts of the region for real operations."

Kryton nodded. The answers were reasonable, and he felt that Levy was trying to be respectful.

"So why did they attack my people? Why the need for so much violence on a training serial?"

Levy shrugged his shoulders.

"They thought you might have been kidnappers, thieves, criminals. Who knows!? They said to me that they were being chased by people they knew not to be part of the training. What would you think in their position?"

Kryton knew that Levy had a point. Cav and Jo had proven that the two agents were up to something nefarious, but had chased them only on the assumption they were linked to Boyd. Levy's explanations countered that narrative nicely. Perhaps too nicely. But the Mossad was still a world class spy agency. Their cover stories would be well drilled.

There was really nothing else Kryton could do. Perhaps it was just a case of operational cross-over. After all, Dubai in the present day is what Berlin was during the Cold War – an oasis of intelligence agencies, diplomats, criminal enterprises, and entrepreneurs all conducting their own activities.

"Excuse me for a moment," said Kryton, leaving Levy and joining Cav and Jo.

"Jonas; thoughts?" he said back to Greyfin HQ, who had been listening in to the entire conversation.

11

Jonas looked around the ops room at the analysts – a clear sign that he wanted input. Any input. None was forthcoming. He ran his hand over the nape of his neck and shrugged.

"I think we're done here. Hand them over," Jonas instructed.

"Roger," replied Kryton, moving back over to where Levy was standing and asking him to follow him into the warehouse.

The pair moved over to the table.

"Okay, time to go," Kryton said to the two sitting agents.

As they walked out into the evening night, Cav spoke to the man who he had fought in the bowels of the shopping mall.

"No hard feelings, okay mate!?" he said, winking.

The agent just looked back at the Australian commando with a scowl on his face, before getting into the SUV.

Cav looked at Jo.

"I tried," he said turning away, likely having already forgotten about it.

Levy ensured that his people were safely in the SUV, then walked back over to Kryton. He extended his hand. Kryton shook it, nodding in respect to his Israeli counterpart.

"You'll have to excuse us, Mister Levy. The Middle East can make us a little wary. We've been fighting terrorists here for the last twenty years," he said.

Levy released his grip, adjusted the glasses on the bridge of his nose as he looked down to the ground, before looking back up at Kryton and smiling.

"Only twenty!?" he mused, before walking back to his ride.

Kryton smirked sheepishly as he quickly remembered that most Israelis often woke daily wondering if today was the day the Jewish state would once again have to fight to the death for its very survival.

As he turned to join his team to prepare to leave the site, Levy spoke to him again from the door of the vehicle.

"We're not your adversary here, Mister Kryton," said the Israeli.

Kryton looked curiously at Levy, then gave an understanding nod. The SUV turned and manoeuvred back around towards the road, then drove away at speed, kicking up the loose sand from the road. He watched it drive away into the distance, before chuckling to himself.

Guess they knew more about us than we expected, he thought to himself after hearing the Israeli use his surname.

He continued to walk over to Cav and Jo.

"Okay, let's collapse here and get back to AMAB. I need a feed."

3

Jo tapped on a few buttons of the computer, trying to establish the audio-visual gateway back to Australia. As was common with most government issued equipment, it had to be manipulated delicately just to get it to do the very thing it had been purchased at the lowest possible price for.

"We up yet?" asked Kryton as he walked into the SCIF with Cav and Dalton – the latter loudly gnawing on a large muffin that he had found in the base's mess that had been intended for the midnight security team's shift change.

Jo looked at the frogman in disgust.

"What? I brought one for you, too," he muffled between bites.

She ignored his gesture and returned to fiddling with the computer equipment. Kryton rolled his eyes as he took his seat at the end of the small table. The air-conditioning of the secure room was a welcome relief after having spent a day in the heat. A minute later, the video of Jonas appeared on the screen.

"You got me there?" he asked.

"Loud and Clear," responded Kryton.

Jonas nodded before commencing the brief.

"Okay, that was a good handover. A safe one is always a good one. What were your thoughts, Zach?"

Kryton cleared his throat as he leaned forward in his seat. He looked down at some prepared notes.

"Their handler – well I suppose we're still assuming he's their handler – he was calm and switched on. He didn't say anything more than he needed to. He was a friendly enough bloke."

"We had the Adgies take some pictures of the vehicle and the people accompanying him. We're sending it by encrypted link now," said Jo.

14

"No worries. We might get something out of that," replied Jonas. "Did he elaborate on what they were doing there?"

"No, as expected," said Kryton. "He maintained it was just a training exercise. I had a bit of a chat with him, but he maintained the party line."

Jonas wrote notes down on paper on his own desk at HQ. Any detail would help build a picture, and help to determine if the Israelis were in fact involved, or if it was just all an incidental occurrence.

"We tried talking to the two agents that Cav and I got into a scrape with. They kept quiet. I actually got the feeling they thought it *was* all just a training exercise, albeit a very realistic one," said Jo.

Kryton looked over at Jo and nodded in agreement. There really was nothing to suggest that it was anything but pure happenstance, and even in the intelligence game, where players are taught not to flippantly write off anything, sometimes the most obvious answer was in fact the correct one.

"Anything from my people?" asked Dalton, wiping the remaining crumbs from his mouth.

"The NSA was the source of the info regarding the agents being Mossad. Details suggest they are run-of-the-mill field officers," replied Jonas.

"Armed? On a training exercise?" asked the American.

"They take their training seriously. They train like they fight. You special forces blokes should know that."

Dalton sat back in his chair and looked at Cav. They both appreciated and understood that approach to training.

"Alright, we could dwell on this all night. Regardless of who they were, the fact remains that we've lost Boyd, and as a result he still remains a threat. Jonas, what's our next move?" asked Kryton.

"I've got everyone here on this, obviously. There are BOLOs out with all relevant agencies, and we're starting to get our reliable sources across the five-eyes group in that part of the world to start asking questions. He can't stay under the radar for too long."

"And what of the scientists under protection. Any closer to working out how they were discovered?" asked Kryton.

"NSA and ASD tentatively believe it was a targeted cyber hack into the CIA database. They think it was a state-sponsored effort, based on how difficult procuring such secured information would have been."

"Once they were placed into asylum, there must always have been the thought that the Russians would try to come after them one day!?" suggested Jo.

"Exactly. So, this information was on an extreme need-to-know basis. The respective supporting intelligence agencies of the countries that these guys were placed in didn't know about their true origins or the existence of other scientists. Only a few inside the CIA were fully aware, and I'm talking Director level. We've got a tiger team doing some brainstorming to come up with some ideas now."

Kryton looked around at each of the team, noticing how each was trying to stifle a yawn. It had been a long few days.

"For you lot now, however, get some rest. It's morning here so we'll be plugging away at this for the day. We'll reconvene late PM our time and have a COA prepared for you," said Jonas.

"Okay. We'll touch base later. Thanks, Jonas," said Kryton, waving to the screen.

Jo terminated the call and looked at Kryton.

"Guess we'll see what they come up with," she said simply.

He nodded and smiled back at her before letting out a deep sigh.

"Get some rest, team. We'll RV at the mess at 0800."

Big smiles appeared on the faces of the two shooters.

"Gym?" suggested Cav.

"See you there in five," responded Dalton enthusiastically.

The two jumped up and sauntered out of the SCIF like two kids hearing the musical chimes of the approaching ice-cream truck.

"Idiots," mumbled Jo, smiling in a curious manner that suggested she still didn't understand the mindset of special forces operators.

After tidying up the SCIF for later use by the ADF staff, the two remaining Greyfin team members walked back out into the evening sky. Kryton looked up at the waning moon and breathed in forcefully. The air, though still warm, was far more comfortable at that time of night.

"What are your thoughts?" said Jo as she stood next to him, taking off her Katmandu jacket that was no longer required outside of the cold air of the SCIF.

He looked at her and raised his eyebrows in thought.

"I don't know…there was just something about those Israelis. I can't quite put my finger on it."

"Perhaps you have watched too many spy movies!" suggested Jo, chuckling.

Kryton smiled.

"Maybe. Well, it doesn't matter now. Hopefully Jonas' team can reacquire Boyd. We need them to. Zero from one isn't a good start to the season."

"C'mon," said Jo, looking to reassure him, "let's grab one of those muffins Clay was scoffing on. They actually looked pretty good."

4

The piercing noise of revving jet engines slowly filled the morning air as the BAE Hawks of the UAE Air Force taxied down the runway. The skilled pilots would spend the morning conducting practice for an upcoming air show.

Kryton smiled as the planes rapidly ascended into the sky, which itself was slowly transitioning from the deep purple of morning twilight into the bright blue that suggested another fine day was on the cards.

He continued walking towards his planned destination: the airside coalition gym. He had woken early with his mind occupied with the likely next steps, so he had decided to hit the weights room.

A session pumping iron had always been good for clarity.

The gym, as expected, was quiet at that time of the morning, so Kryton settled in to build a sweat.

Over the next twenty minutes, a few more personnel joined him as they commenced their own sessions. Kryton was finishing another set on the squat rack when he heard a voice from nearby.

"Isn't that bad for your knees?"

He turned his head as he placed the bar back onto the rack.

Looking at him and smiling was a familiar face.

"Jesus. How are you, Rick?" said Kryton, extending his hand to a fellow intelligence sergeant – and his long-time friend – Rick Oates.

"Good mate. What are you doing over here? Didn't they boot you out of the green?"

Kryton wiped his brow as he leaned against the rack.

"Yeah. They got desperate and called me back to tidy up some loose ends, though. What are you doing here?"

18

"I got asked to help out on a planning team with the SASR lads. Just travelling through the Middle East and some parts of Africa. We flew in from Perth yesterday, and head out again tonight."

Kryton nodded and understood Rick's role. He, too, had been part of multiple Special Operations Planning Teams – or SOPTs – who travelled globally to undertake on-the-ground reconnaissance to develop standing plans for locations that might require hostage recovery of Australian citizens abroad.

The two experienced professionals, who had first met on their initial intelligence course years earlier, spent a few minutes catching up on old times. Oates then leaned in, conducting the cursory glance over his shoulder that suggested he was going to change the subject to something more sensitive.

"Rumour has it that a new, highly classified special mission unit has been developed, working with the yanks and operating with limited oversight. You wouldn't know anything about that, would you?"

Kryton just shrugged his shoulders.

"Where did you hear that?"

"I was in the Sergeants Mess at Canungra a few weeks back. The RSM was harping on about some secret training activity he was part of that involved all sorts of agencies."

Kryton had a quick flashback to the ORE on the Gold Coast a few weeks earlier, and to one of the serials where he had deliberately put a few extra simunition rounds, at close range, into one of the enemy role players.

The protective mask might have concealed his identity, but the rotund figure made it very clear that the player was one of Kryton's former superiors from earlier in his career. A superior who had tried to throw the junior intelligence soldier under the bus when a special forces mission had gone wrong due to bad intelligence, resulting in the wounding of several shooters, even though that brief had been prepared by the now senior warrant officer.

Kryton hadn't been surprised that the incompetent, overweight man had made it to the highest position an enlisted soldier could make within his beloved corps. After all, the man had spent a career leveraging other people's successes and delegating his own failures. Kryton had served under many brilliant warrant officers throughout his career, but there were a few who let the integrity of the corps down.

He was even less surprised that that RSM had been shooting his mouth off in the mess. Fortunately, he was confident that the probably very few people who were even bothering to listen to him would show much more discretion.

"I do whatever they need me to do," said Kryton nonchalantly.

Oates smiled and nodded, impressed.

"Well, I'm glad to see that you're back in the game, mate. Grab a brew later before I go?"

"Yeah, I'd like that," said Kryton.

Oates gave the thumbs up, then proceeded to re-join his team at the bench press in the corner, clearly distinguished by their reversed baseball hats and bushy beards. Kryton finished his session and headed back to the transit room he was sharing with Cav and Dalton. He was passing through he accommodation area when Jo called out his name. He turned to see her running in his direction.

"Morni..." was about all he could say out loud before she interrupted him.

"You better come quickly. There's been a development," she informed him.

It seemed serious.

"What is it?"

She was about to speak, but two passing uniformed soldiers made her pause.

"Not here. SCIF," she said.

"Can I grab a quick shower?"

She looked at him up and down, only now really noticing his PT clothing and the sweaty towel around his shoulders. She didn't particularly relish the idea of sitting in a windowless room with him in his current state.

"Ah, yeah. Okay, twenty minutes. Jonas will update us. Bring the other ones, too, if they're even awake yet."

He nodded at her and turned to jog off. Less than fifteen minutes later, the three men swiped their access cards and joined Jo in the SCIF. Jonas' image was once again on the screen. His tie was loosened and his collar undone.

"Wow, mate. You look knackered," said Kryton.

Jonas looked up to the camera in his small office at Greyfin's HQ in Canberra.

"Yeah, it's been a bloody long day. I hope you all got some rest, 'cos we have a new task."

This grabbed the attention of the team, so they took a seat around the table and leaned in, ready to receive the brief from Jonas.

"Alright, let's go. After Volkov was killed, the CIA tried to secure the other four scientists who were in the asylum deal. They hoped that they might have some info regarding who Boyd actually is."

"And?" asked Kryton.

"And, it's a cluster. Three of them are missing, and we just got word that a fourth has been discovered by a field team from the CIA Special Activities Division tasked to secure him."

They all looked at each other, intrigued by the evolving situation.

"Well, isn't *that* a win at least?" asked Cav.

"No, it isn't. He's dead. The report from the SAD team said he was murdered in his apartment in Munich."

"Germany!?" exclaimed Dalton.

Jonas nodded. It seemed that the Americans had spread the scientists all over the world. Kryton thought it strange that they had placed a high-value witness in western Europe, considering its relative proximity to Russia. However, he knew that sometimes it was easier to hide someone close to where you could actually watch them, and the U.S. still had a strong military and intelligence presence in Germany.

"When? When was he murdered?" he asked Jonas.

"Indications are that it was probably two or three days ago," said Jonas. "The CIA pulled the SAD team to get them to start on the trail of the others, but we've been advised that there is very little to go off of. It's like they've just vanished."

"Do you think they knew about Volkov and went into hiding?" asked Jo.

"It's a possibility. The CIA kept their respective locations close hold and assigned different case officers to monitor them. However, keep in mind that these are smart men. They could have had any number of communication methods and procedures set up amongst themselves before they went into protection which we're not privy to."

The team sitting around the small desk looked at each other. They were all unsure as to what this actually meant for their mission, which at this point appeared dead in the water.

"Sooo…do we go home then?" asked Cav.

"Negative," replied Jonas. "Zach, you and Jo will head to Munich to see what intelligence you can gather, if any. We'll send the SAD debrief to you in-flight."

"Our cover and point-of-contact?" asked Kryton.

"You'll maintain the AFP cover, hence it's just the two of you. The embassy in Berlin will make arrangements for you to RV with a yet-to-be-determined person. The guise is we've got an interest in the dead guy based on drug shipments into South-East Asia."

"Not much of a legacy for the poor bloke, is it?" said Kryton.

"I doubt they'll be conducting any obituaries for him," mentioned Jo.

Kryton nodded and smiled. The man had – whether by choice or not – given up any previous life the moment he had sought asylum from the Americans.

"Rightio. We continue on. What about these two?" asked Kryton, motioning to Cav and Dalton.

The two shooters leaned forward, keen to hear their own taskings.

"Well, if they don't mind, they will stay and continue to enjoy the AMAB hospitality for a few days yet."

Both Cav and Dalton slumped in their chairs. No soldier liked being left behind.

"I hear that there's a beach volleyball tournament tomorrow!" said Kryton, in an insincere attempt to put a positive spin on the situation.

"Perhaps a trip to Dubai for some shopping might be in order," said Jo jokingly to Dalton. "That shirt is just... wow."

As the others in the team started to stand at the conclusion of the brief, Dalton looked down at the bright red, short sleeved bowling shirt that he was wearing, genuinely confused as to what the issue with it was.

"My mother gave this to me," he responded feebly.

5

The Gulfstream G650 jet made a slight adjustment of course and commenced its climb to 35,000 feet at the behest of Italian air traffic control. The pilot barely needed to touch the throttle before the technologically advanced aircraft responded to his light touch.

The air traffic over this part of the world – a major thoroughfare between Europe and the Middle East – required the utmost of consideration as to the placement of the hundreds of aircraft movements daily, and placing the small jet at a higher altitude would allow the much larger passenger airlines to travel with relative impunity.

The young tin pusher based in Rome would think nothing of the small plane that was ostensibly registered to an innocuous private holdings company based in the Caribbean, and likely carrying some wealthy CEO to their next meeting.

Kryton looked out of the small framed window and down at the reflection of the sun glistening off of the beautiful blue water below. He again squeezed the armrests of the plush swivel chair he sat in, perhaps for the fifth or sixth time of the trip. The smell of fresh leather and mahogany finishes on the internal fittings overwhelmed the ex-paratrooper, who was far used to less refined travel.

The CIA sure know how to travel, he thought to himself.

"You all good?" asked Jo from the chair adjacent to him, whilst looking at him curiously.

"Yeah, why?" he replied.

"You've had a stupid Cheshire cat grin on your face since we took off," she said, smiling.

He sat up a little more upright in the seat and sat still for a moment before replying.

"Just enjoying the ambience."

Jo looked around the cabin, shrugged her shoulders, and put her head back down into her laptop. He looked at her, rolled his eyes, and returned his gaze back out the window. Sure, she might have been used to first class travel. The joke had always been that half the annual ASIS budget went towards exorbitant airline tickets. He, on the other hand, was used to no such luxuries, and was going to take a moment to enjoy the experience.

Not for too long, though. He got up from his chair and moved over next to Jo.

"What do we have?"

She turned the laptop slightly so he could see what she had been working on. A mug shot of a rather average looking Caucasian man was displayed on the screen – part of the top-secret dossier the Greyfin analysts had been provided by the CIA.

"Vladimir Smirnov, AKA Joseph Fischer. One of the nuclear scientists who was placed in protective asylum by the CIA; no family; highly qualified; apparently, he had been working at the German equivalent of a TAFE teaching basic engineering."

"Why did they put him in Germany?" pondered Kryton loudly.

Jo scrolled down the dossier at the notes on the now dead man.

"Ummm...because he spoke German," she said simply, not finding any notes outlining otherwise.

"Oh, well that makes sense, I guess," deadpanned Kryton.

The reasons didn't really matter anyway. Their job was simply to try to see if there was anything that would provide them intelligence on what was fast becoming a dead end. Boyd was still the target – the only known entity in a severely compromised highly classified protection operation that had now claimed two victims.

The highest levels of government had now prioritised this effort, haunted by the prospect of yet another major intelligence failure. If it became common knowledge that highly valued intelligence assets had been killed whilst in protection, then western agencies for many years to come could kiss goodbye the prospect of foreigners willing to risk everything to betray their own nation.

That's why it was so important to find out who was behind the killings, and how they had come to know where the scientists were being kept. Kryton was not convinced that the trip to Munich would yield significant results, but he knew that it was always wise to err on the side of caution and leave no stone unturned, just in case.

Several hours later, after flying over the majestic edge of the Swiss Alps, the luxury jet landed at the Munich International Airport. The small Gulfstream looked tiny as it taxied amongst the much larger international airline carriers. The sun had recently set, and the airport lights twinkled in the evening twilight.

The pilot brought the plane to a halt on the corporate jet apron, well away from the hustle and bustle of the domestic and international terminals. Living cover meant going through the proper motions, and Kryton joined Jo on the tarmac as the officer from German Immigration conducted the required customs checks.

Approximately thirty minutes later, the two of them were in a taxi and heading to their pre-booked hotel in downtown Munich. It was late, and there would be little that could be achieved tonight with the German authorities.

Kryton kept an enthusiastic eye out of the window as the taxi drove through the rural outer suburbs and into the denser area of the Bavarian capital. The traffic was still gridlocked as commuters made their way home, scattered amongst the young people and tourists alike who were heading out to enjoy the nice evening weather.

"Cav and Dalton will be mad. They think that there is a beer hall on every corner and that Oktoberfest is an everyday event," said Jo.

Kryton laughed.

"I doubt it's a missed opportunity," he replied, although as the taxi drew closer to the hotel it did actually appear that there was an above average number of drinking establishments for a large city. "Oh well. Let's just tell them that it was rather disappointing on the beer front."

Jo smiled and looked back out of the window, also enjoying seeing a new city for the first time. The driver soon pulled into the front of the Mandarin Oriental Hotel, one of Munich's finest abodes. Kryton was taken aback as a young, well-dressed man opened the door.

"Good evening, sir," said the hotel doorman in a distinct Bavarian accent as he waited for the Australian to alight from the vehicle.

"Yeah, umm, g'day mate. Thanks," said Kryton, standing like a kangaroo caught in headlights by the unexpected VIP treatment.

Jo — being much more attuned to the expectations of executive service — walked around to join Kryton.

"Danke. Sehr geschatzt," she said, thanking the doorman and placing a small tip in his hand.

She looked at Kryton, smiled, and just shook her head before attending to the bags. Kryton quickly shrugged off the feeling of foolishness and looked up at the magnificent façade of the hotel. The architecture of the building nestled in a corner position of the famed Maximilian Strasse had to be seen to be believed. He smiled.

Now *this* was the James Bond lifestyle he had expected when joining army intelligence. One that, in reality, had turned out to have been quite the opposite.

Better late than never, he thought.

He walked inside and joined Jo. Ten minutes later, the two Australian spies were getting comfortable in the lush two-bedroom suite.

"Dinner in ten? I'm just having a shower," said Jo.

"No worries," replied Kryton, still trying to determine if he was more fascinated by the selections in the mini bar, or by the two-headed shower in his own ensuite.

He was just about to have his own shower when he heard a large rattling on the door. He cautiously approached it, curious as to who would be on the other side, especially since they weren't expecting company.

He peered through the peephole, and saw another smartly dressed doorman standing neatly with a metal tray in his hand. Kryton opened the door and looked down at the scrawny teenager standing in front of him.

"Herr Kryton?" asked the young man.

"Umm...Ja," replied the Australian, drawing upon the limited German he had learnt from every war movie he had ever seen.

The young doorman held the tray up to Kryton. A beige envelope was on it. Kryton took hold of it, and before he could thank him, the young man quickly turned and walked off.

"Okay, then," mumbled Kryton, turning around and locking the door behind him.

He examined the envelope carefully. There was no addressee printed on it, just the room number. He decided there was only one way to find out its contents, so he opened it and pulled out a folded, single A4 sheet of paper.

He unfolded it and read it closely.

Superintendent Hans Brenninger.
0900.
Bavarian Police – Ministry of the Interior (Hof Garten).

26

He re-folded the sheet of paper and looked around the room for a map. Sitting on a coffee table was exactly what he was looking for – a local tourist guide. He opened it up and quickly worked out where the hotel was in relation to the station.

"Nice one, Jonas," he said quietly as he worked out that the hotel was within walking distance of the police station.

That would make navigating the rather maze like city much easier. He placed the paper back into the envelope. Despite all the technology they had access to, he thought that there was something cool and old school about being on an intelligence operation and receiving a sealed message on arrival to the hotel.

"Just like Bond," he chuckled to himself.

6

Kryton and Jo sat in the foyer of the police station, waiting to meet with their contact, Superintendent Brenninger. The building was a hive of activity, and it appeared that the overnight shift was being swapped out by the officers who would undertake the day beat.

A nearby door abruptly opened, and a tall, well-built, and well-dressed man purposely strode out and towards the front desk. Wearing a dark three-piece suit with a dark maroon tie, he quietly spoke to the seated uniformed officer, who proceeded to point to where the two Australians were sitting.

Kryton and Jo stood as the man walked over to them, extending his large hand.

"Guten morgen, I am Hans Brenninger," said the plain clothed officer enthusiastically, with a large smile and in a thick regional accent.

"Good morning, sir, I am Zach Kryton," said the intelligence operator, shaking Brenninger's hand whilst displaying his AFP badge with the other one.

Brenninger looked down at Jo. Her jaw was loosely ajar as she looked back up at the imposing man, whose accent and frame instantly reminded her of Arnold Schwarzenegger.

"Uh, my name is Jo," she said, finding his handshake to be firm but gentle.

The German officer nodded and stood back, slightly turning his body and raising his arm towards the door he had just come out of.

"Would you please come this way?" he said kindly.

Kryton and Jo followed Brenninger down a hallway and into the interior of the station. Kryton was impressed with how neat and well laid out the office was. Most of the police stations he had been in looked like a bomb had gone off in it.

German efficiency at its best, he thought to himself.

They continued to follow Brenninger through the hallways until they reached his office. It was just as neat as the rest of the building, with a small table in the corner, and a large mahogany desk with a large leather-bound chair taking pride of place in the centre.

Kryton quickly reviewed the contents of the office – an old habit that spooks form early in their careers. A small framed photo sat in the corner of the desk, suggesting that Brenninger was a family man with two pretty teenage daughters. The walls were adorned with various other photos, most containing Brenninger at various stages of his obviously eclectic career. Kryton recognised the weapons and tactical equipment in one particular photo, and he moved in to look at it more closely.

"You served in GSG-9?" asked Kryton.

Brenninger smiled and nodded.

"You recognise our tactical unit?"

Kryton responded with a slight nod as he continued to look at the photos.

"I was in the army before I went on to join the feds. We had a few of your men do a short-term exchange with us once. Very good operators."

Brenninger smiled in appreciation, then gestured for his two guests to take a seat around the table. Kryton had to hide a smirk as he remembered the night that most of the members of 2nd Commando Regiment's Tactical Assault Group took their German exchange officers to an Adelaide strip club, and proceeded to get so drunk that they had to be poured into a taxi to return to base for the following day's exercises.

But that was a story for another time. For now, the focus was on the present. He took a seat at the table as Brenninger sat back into the chair, giving his visitors his full attention.

"So, I've been told that you wish to know about our case regarding Mister Fischer."

Kryton leaned in and cleared his throat.

"Well, yes sir. Fischer was on our wanted list as being part of a large criminal operation smuggling heroin through Thailand and into Australia. Our intelligence suggested that he was in middle management, if not a regional leader of the cartel which, we believe, may have South American links," said Kryton, outlining a well-planned cover story.

The German officer listened closely, before opening a file on the desk in front of him.

"I must admit, this comes as a surprise to us," he said as he rifled through the paperwork within the homicide file. "He has no criminal past here in Germany."

Kryton looked at Jo nervously. The Greyfin analyst team were supposed to have been setting up a digital trail that would support the cover story. It was obvious that Brenninger was a smart individual, and he would easily find any gaps.

"Umm…well, we had the Red Notice placed through INTERPOL," said Jo.

Brenninger sifted through some more of the pages, then pulled one freshly printed sheet to the surface of the file.

"Ahh, here's something. Yes, he was indeed wanted for drug trafficking on this notice. Apparently, he was originally from Austria. No details on any other previous movements or criminal activity, however. We're still talking to our border control to determine his immigration status."

"In my experience, the best traffickers deliberately lead the quietest life," said Kryton, hoping to delay Brenninger from inevitably looking too in depth into the CIA created artificial background of the dead scientist before he and Jo had a chance to achieve their aim.

"Yes, of course, you're right," responded the German in agreement.

"Would you mind if we viewed the body, if only to confirm identity for our own investigations?" asked Kryton.

Brenninger thought for a moment, then closed the file and looked up at them. He nodded and smiled.

"That won't be a problem," he said, standing and gesturing for Kryton and Jo to once again follow him.

A few minutes later, they were in a cold and austere room that was the Munich city morgue. A lone officer wearing medical overalls greeted Brenninger, and the two had a quick conversation in German. The two Australians followed their host over to a numbered mortuary cabinet.

"It should be this one," said Brenninger as he opened the door and heaved on the large tray, pulling it out from its cold, dark recess.

Jo baulked a little as Brenninger nonchalantly peeled back the head covering, exposing the lifeless figure lying face up on the tray.

Kryton had no such reactions – he had seen enough death to last a lifetime, and as far as he was concerned this was just another part of the job. He stepped in closer to examine the body in front of him.

The former Russian scientist matched his profile both in terms of height and appearance. Despite the trauma the body had been through, Kryton thought that he actually looked younger than his sixty years. The only difference to his face from the file image was the small, perfectly formed hole in the centre of his forehead – the obvious entry point of a small calibre bullet.

"If I may ask, what is your early assessment of the case?" Kryton asked Brenninger.

The German officer turned his head slightly to look down at the corpse, then exhaled deeply.

"Until we heard from your people, our assumption was that it was just a robbery gone wrong. His apartment was a mess, but he may have just lived that way. Clearly, cause of death is by shooting as you can see..."

Brenninger was cut off by the sound of the main door to the refrigeration unit opening and one of his officers calling out to him in German.

"Excuse me, I'll be back in a moment," he said politely, before moving off to deal with the intrusion.

Kryton nodded, then turned his attention back to the body. Jo, now acclimatised to the scene before her, moved to the other side of the tray and also looked down at the dead Russian.

"I always find dead bodies creepy," she whispered.

"You've seen too many horror movies," he replied.

Kryton looked up and could see that Brenninger was engaged in conversation with his subordinate.

"Move a little to your left," he quietly said to Jo, seeking to become obscured from Brenninger's view.

Jo did so, her curiosity as to why being answered as Kryton lowered the sheet covering the body even further down and exposing the naked corpse.

"Zach, no..." she protested softly, until she saw two additional holes, of the same size as the one in the forehead, situated in the middle of the chest.

"This was a professional hit," said Kryton confidently.

"Are you sure?" asked Jo.

Kryton pointed to the entry wounds in the Russian's body.

"Two rounds in the chest, one in the head. Special operations soldiers get taught various techniques to rapidly engage multiple targets at close range using two rounds per target, but assassins use three rounds to ensure a kill, because they have the luxury of time when engaging a single target."

"So, these guys *are* being assassinated," observed Jo, with their suspicions appearing to be confirmed.

"It looks that way," replied Kryton, who then placed the cover back into its original position.

"What do you think the German's thoughts are?" she asked him.

"Well, Brenninger served in GSG-9. He'll know a professional hit when he sees one. The drug trafficking narrative actually provides a motive for the assassination, so they will suspect it's a fight between some cartel or another organised crime group. I'm unsure of the drug supply situation here in Munich, but I suspect our new German friend will get his team to start kicking some doors in very soon," said Kryton as he motioned towards Brenninger.

The sounds of the main door closing interrupted their conversation, and Brenninger quickly re-joined them next to the body.

"Where was I? Oh, yes. Cause of death was obvious as you can see. We think that this was a targeted killing. We'd be interested to know what more you can tell us about him. To be honest with you, we don't have any leads at the moment."

"No witnesses or any CCTV footage?" asked Jo.

"I am afraid not. This is a relatively safe part of the city, and none of the neighbours had cameras set up outside of their homes. It looks like this was done during the night. One of the neighbours reported last seeing him in the afternoon."

Kryton thought for a moment. The grouping of the bullet holes aside, this was showing all the hallmarks of a well planned and executed hit. Whoever did it must have known Smirnov's routine, and was able to get in and out without rousing suspicion.

"Do you think we might be able to look at his apartment?" asked Kryton. "I'd be happy to fill you in on the details I'm permitted to share, in order to help your case," he added.

Kryton hadn't spent the entire flight relaxing in the plush chairs of the Gulfstream. Both he and Jo had read in detail the cover story prepared by the Greyfin analysts, knowing that questions would be asked of them by the Germans surrounding the dead scientist's identity and associates. Perfectly reasonable questions in line with their investigation, but questions that the Australians would have to be able to answer to ensure their cover story held up, and which would hopefully make the Germans agree to allow them have the access to the crime scene they were now seeking.

"Certainly. I can take you out there now if you like?" suggested Brenninger.

7

Veroneser Street
Suburban Munich
Sixty minutes later

The unmarked police BMW turned the corner into a quiet and narrow suburban street. The majority of the residential houses were fronted by large, green hedges, and old-style Bavarian architecture mingled amongst the more modern German designs.

Kryton had spent the journey sharing false details with Brenninger – mostly innocuous detail that was mostly true, such as details about illegal drug operations in the Indo-Pacific region, but nothing that would not stand up to any further scrutiny, and all of which would lead any subsequent German investigation to a dead end.

Brenninger pulled up in front of a small house with a white picket fence. Police tape cordoned off the house, but otherwise the street looked peaceful. The distant noise of players shouting echoed across the street, as players from the famous FC Bayern soccer club practiced for their next Bundesliga match at their nearby headquarters. By doctrine, the CIA had done well by hiding Smirnov in a typical, non-descript suburban street. The scientist had every reason to believe he would be safe in his asylum.

Not well enough, however, as it had turned out.

Brenninger pulled the vehicle next to the curb on the other side of the street. Its three occupants disembarked and walked towards the house, ducking under the police tape and walking towards the front door.

A uniformed officer standing guard acknowledged his superior, who motioned for Kryton and Jo to follow him inside. They proceeded through the front door and immediately up a set of stairs. Kryton realised that the house was in fact two small apartments. He made sure to take careful note of the structure of the building. There were no signs of forced entry, either at the main door or at the door to the rather non-

34

descript apartment where Smirnov had been killed. Brenninger gently pushed the door open and stepped inside, turning on a light switch. A dull, single globe flickered for a second before turning on completely, but it was of barely enough wattage to illuminate the room.

Kryton stepped inside the apartment and took a moment to look around. It certainly didn't look like a *home* per say, but more like a transit room that actually reminded him of some of the accommodation blocks at military bases back in Australia that non-married soldiers lived in. The type that had nothing more than the basics – a single bed; a small ensuite; and, a kitchenette that would never do more than allow an occupant to heat up meals in a microwave.

He noticed that the blinds were closed. He walked over to the window and peered through them to outside. All of the windows were bolted shut. It was at that point he realised how musty the apartment was. It was obvious that it hadn't seen any fresh air for some time.

"Is this where you found the body?" asked Jo, pointing to a large reclining chair in the corner of the room.

"Yes, it is," replied the German officer. "It appeared that he was sitting back having a cup of tea and reading the newspaper, based on how we found his body. We have taken those items in for forensic testing. Who knows, we might find something."

Kryton walked over and looked down at the chair, then turned to face the apartment's door. He wasn't a trained investigator, but as an intelligence operator he had been trained to think like one; trained to try and put himself in the shoes of the opposition.

"What do you think?" asked Jo, noting the thoughts racing through her colleague's head.

Kryton sighed, then waked over to the door. Remnants of the fine powder used by forensic scientists to pull fingerprints off of surfaces covered the door knob.

"Have you found any other fingerprints?" he asked.

Brenninger looked up from his phone.

"No. Nothing at all."

"Nothing? Not even a third person's ones?"

Brenninger just shook his head.

"I think our victim led a very reclusive and basic life. If it wasn't for you telling us about his secret side hustle, we would have probably had to shelve this case almost immediately."

Kryton saw his opportunity.

35

"Well, in that case, do you mind if we have access to some of the evidence?" he asked.

Brenninger looked at the Australian for a moment. Not out of suspicion – after all, it was a perfectly reasonable request from one law enforcement officer to another – but mostly because it appeared like he was thinking about whether he had the authority to make such a decision.

He started nodding slowly and smiled reluctantly.

"I am sorry, but I will have to seek approval for such a request. I'm sure it won't be a problem; however, we will have to follow the process, you understand?"

Kryton smiled and nodded.

That German efficiency again, he thought to himself.

"Of course, please. Happy to provide whatever you might need."

"If you'll excuse me, I'll step outside and make a call. Please be careful in here; it's still an active crime scene and we want to keep it undisturbed for now."

Jo stepped aside to allow Brenninger to leave the apartment. She turned to look at Kryton, still seeking an answer to her previously asked question.

"Well, what do you think?" she repeated.

He looked at her and apologised, realising he had been so caught up in his own thoughts that he had left her original question hanging.

"He lived like a person ready to leave here at a moments notice. The lack of furniture; the closed-up apartment; that bag next to the door by your feet. I bet you that's a go-bag," he said.

Jo looked down at the previously unseen object. It was a medium size leather carry bag with handles tucked neatly to the side. Its bulkiness suggested it was full.

"Perhaps he liked the dark," she suggested unconvincingly.

Kryton chuckled.

"Maybe. I think he never quite felt safe in hiding, and was probably just waiting for the day someone would come knocking," he said.

"Seems like that day has come," Jo lamented. "Do you think he let the person in or did the assassin pick the lock?"

Kryton let out a deep sigh, once again thinking deeply.

"Based on the way the apartment was set-up, I doubt he would have let a person in, returned to his chair, and then sat enjoying a brew and a conversation."

He quickly moved to the window, pulled the blind aside slightly, and looked down to see Brenninger still talking on his phone on the street. He then turned and walked over to Jo, gently grabbing her arm and escorting her over to the apartment's door.

"Zach…what on Earth are you…" she protested.

"Stand here. Let me know if they come back up," he said softly.

He then pulled a pair of latex gloves out of his jacket pocket and put them on quickly. He then knelt down and opened the bag, rifling through it briskly. Finding only some spare clothing and a wad of Euros neatly tucked into a plastic covered manila envelope, he shut the bag and returned it to its original position, being careful to ensure even the handles sat appropriately.

Jo looked at him, both frustrated and confused.

"What are you doing?" she asked firmly.

He stood up and quickly looked back around the room.

"The CIA put him in here, right?" he asked.

"Yeah, that's right."

"Well, it's likely they taught him some basic tradecraft; for example, how to hide sensitive details regarding how he could be in contact with them should the need arise."

Jo smiled and nodded. Kryton got back down on his hands and knees, looking under the chair and table in the small kitchen, and carefully opening the draws and brushing his hand on the undersides.

He found nothing.

"Brenninger said in the car that he hadn't consulted with any other agencies, didn't he?" Kryton asked Jo.

"Umm…yeah. Why?"

"And Jonas said that the intelligence agencies in each of the countries that the scientists were placed were made aware of the action, if only vaguely," he also queried, continuing his search and still unsure of what he was actually looking for.

Jo kept one eye out the door and down the stairs.

"That's correct. But he also said that they weren't aware of the other scientists in the other countries."

"So, do you think German intelligence isn't even aware that Smirnov is dead yet?" asked Kryton.

"I would think not. Jonas never mentioned anything about the CIA having told them. I think it would be too embarrassing, for both the CIA and the Germans."

Kryton nodded in agreement. He then eyed off a small narrow bookshelf in the opposite corner of the room from where the chair Smirnov had been killed in was. He ran his gloved hand over a series of old looking books. Some were in German; others English; whilst one particular one caught Kryton's attention. He slowly pulled it out. It looked like some fictional novel, which he conservatively estimated was about 300 pages in length.

"What is it?" asked Jo nervously, concerned that their meddling would be discovered at any moment.

Kryton held the book up and smiled at her.

"No dust on this one."

He carefully opened it, examining the interior for any loose documents. He then gently grasped the back of the hard covered book and opened it widely, almost folding it back upon itself. He noticed a small cut in the spine. Not a tear from negligent care of the book, but something manmade.

Kryton gently prodded the pages to open the cut even further, and shifted the angle to make better use of the limited light. He could see something inside. He turned the book over and gently tapped it on the shelf. Almost immediately a small rectangular object popped out and almost bounced off of the shelf. Kryton instinctively reached out and grabbed it. He opened his hand, and was now looking at the small item.

"What have you got?" asked Jo curiously, having walked over to stand next to Kryton.

"It's a sim card or something," he replied, twisting it between his fingers.

"No. That's a micro-SD card. Good for data storage," she informed him.

"Good for hiding, too" he responded, winking at her like he had just struck gold.

The distinct sounds of footsteps on creaking wood alerted them to an imminent disturbance. Jo moved to the door to buy Kryton the valuable few seconds needed to return the book back to its original position and calmly slip the SD card into his pocket. By the time Brenninger made it to the top of the stairs, Kryton was already standing next to Jo, having removed and tucked away the latex gloves into his jacket.

"Did you find anything that might help with your investigation?" Brenninger politely asked the two of them.

Kryton shook his head, feigning disappointment.

"I'm afraid not. Like you said earlier, he lived a very austere existence. How did you go with your superiors?"

"Yes, that will not be a problem. I will need you to come and sign some paperwork; it's mostly international agency sharing arrangements and so on," replied Brenninger.

"Thank you, we appreciate it," said Jo.

Brenninger motioned for his two guests to exit the apartment. Once they departed, he gently closed the door behind them and proceeded down the stairs. Kryton gave an appreciative nod to the uniformed guard at the entrance to the house.

"What exactly is it you were hoping you would find?" asked Brenninger as they walked back to the BMW.

Another fair question, and one the two Australians readily had an answer for.

"Well, mostly we wanted to identify the body and confirm that it was our person. We thought maybe your investigation might yield some leads that we could leverage off," said Kryton.

"Well, we're still in the early stages of the investigation, so I'm sure we'll uncover more as we look to interview some of his colleagues at his workplace, and look into his banking and digital records. We'll keep you informed as appropriate."

"We appreciate that, too," said Kryton.

They stopped at the doors of the BMW. Brenninger looked over the roof at Kryton standing on the other side.

"My commanders are interested in your drug affiliation lines of inquiry. Would you be happy to share any details that *we* could leverage off? To assist in our investigation, of course."

Kryton had to hide a smile. Brenninger had been very polite, but it was obvious that he was also very smart. This was his way of saying 'we'll help you, but what's in it for us?' He respected that.

"Naturally."

Brenninger nodded. The simple one-word answer was Kryton's way of showing that respect. Most soldiers and intelligence operators didn't say more than was absolutely needed, and the Australian considered Brenninger a colleague deserving of it.

The two men joined Jo inside the vehicle.

"We will return to the station and I can show you some of the forensic evidence. There's not much to be honest; it's mainly DNA we're examining for, unless there is something in particular that is of interest to you?" said Brenninger.

"You never know. We could get lucky," said Kryton as he fastened his seatbelt.

Brenninger slowly adjusted the gears of the luxury vehicle and pulled out into the street.

"How long will you be staying in Munich for? There's a street festival on this week," said the German, changing to a lighter subject.

Kryton pursed his lips and shook his head.

"I'm afraid we'll have to miss it," said Jo from the rear seat, with a tinge of genuine disappointment in her voice. "We're on a flight back to Australia this evening."

8

Kryton wiped the sweat off of his brow as he commenced the last part of his 10-kilometre run. He nodded at the small group of USAF personnel who ran past him in formation in the opposite direction. He couldn't help but admire the way they maintained cadence, but did wonder if the fitter people in the group actually got anything out of the exercise if they had to slow down to the pace of the less aerobically inclined.

He had risen before dawn to go for a run. He felt rested enough after sleeping for the majority of the flight back from Munich – a luxury that hadn't been afforded to Jo, who had spent the flight sending the contents of the SD card they had found in Smirnov's small apartment back to Canberra over encrypted channels.

He took in a long, deep breath and extended his stride in order to increase his speed. He was pleased with how his knees had held up in the run, no doubt in part due to the compression pants he was wearing – a recommendation from his physiotherapist back in Australia.

Kryton had initially baulked at the idea, feeling that it made him look like a ballet dancer; but after a few runs in the deliberately constricting material, he had wondered why he'd spent so many years pounding the pavement without them. By the time he was 500 metres out from the front gate to the Australian compound, he was close to sprinting.

The sound of a revving engine soon pierced the morning sky, and he could see a UAE Air Force BAE-Hawk commence its acceleration down the runway in preparation for take-off. The road leading towards the entrance of the front gate ran parallel to the runway, and Kryton smiled as he found a little extra spring in his step as he tried to keep pace with it.

He felt that he had the plane covered for the first 100 metres, until the British manufactured jet engine picked up pace and went tearing down the runway. Kryton continued sprinting right up to the gate, and stopped to watch the plane ascend almost vertically into the orange glow of the morning sky.

He was blowing heavily, and kicked himself for trying to sprint in the already hot air. A few deep breaths brought his heartrate back down, and he pulled his identification card from his pocket and held it up to the RAAF airman who was conducting sentry duties in the guardhouse. The young man smiled at Kryton as he pressed the button to unlock the hessian covered gate.

Kryton walked through and headed towards his accommodation hut. The compound was abuzz as the day workers commenced their morning. Many were in their PT clothing, whilst others were in their Australian Camouflage Military Unforms – or ACMU – with their respective services only distinguished by the small flags velcroed onto their upper arms.

Kryton jogged up the small set of stairs and into his hut at the rear of the compound in an area assigned to special forces units and members of other government agencies. He walked down the air-conditioned hallway and into his room. The building was quiet, with the members of the SOPT having departed on their mission a day earlier. He gently opened the door and was immediately greeted by the sound of two bodies snoring loudly, almost as if they were competing with each other.

He just rolled his eyes and walked over to his bunk space, switching on a small light above his bed. The snoring was replaced by a grunt as one of the bodies roused from its slumber. The nauseating sound of a throat being cleared made Kryton wince. He turned around to see Dalton rubbing his eyes.

"Morning, sunshine," whispered the Australian.

The SEAL yawned and opened his eyes to examine his surroundings.

"Oh, hey Zach. When did you get back?"

"A few hours ago. I've been up and gone for a run and everything."

He grabbed his towel off of the rack and turned to look for his toiletries bag.

"What did you two get up to while I was away?"

The American sat up in his bed.

"We had a few drinks with some of the girls from AusAID," he said, referring to the Australian Government run humanitarian aid organisation.

"Oh yeah. Any luck?" asked Kryton.

"Well, we're back in here alone, aren't we!"

Kryton shrugged his shoulders.

"Next time, maybe," he said.

Having swapped out his running shoes for a pair of thongs, he made his way back towards the door.

"Get this one up, will you?" he said, motioning towards the sprawled-out body of Cav. "We've got a brief at 0900."

"Any luck in Germany?" asked Dalton.

"Dunno yet. We got something, it's just a matter of what."

Dalton looked at him with some confusion on his face. Kryton smiled and winked at the frogman.

"I'll see you in the mess for brekky."

He gently closed the door and walked outside and towards the shower block. The locally hired staff were busy conducting their daily cleaning duties and taking care of the beautifully manicured gardens. He had been through AMAB on numerous occasions whilst on various deployments, yet he still found it fascinating that the Australian Government would spend so much money on making the compound look like an expensive university college, resplendent with flower beds and neatly trimmed lawns. The air-conditioning bill alone must have chewed up a considerable amount of the budget, considering some of them had probably been continuously operating for years.

Anyway, he had other things to focus on.

Kryton indulged himself with a few extra minutes under the water as he took his shower. In his mind he went over the past few weeks, looking at multiple scenarios as to why the scientists were being killed off, and more importantly, who was behind it all. The odds were still with it being the Russians looking to get revenge on their absconding scientists. That seemed even more likely given two of them were now dead, having been assassinated on opposite ends of the globe. Only a state actor would have the resources to do that. He sincerely hoped that the SD card would yield something, because if it didn't, they were pretty much at another dead end.

He finished his shower, and twenty minutes later he was freshly dressed in civilian clothes and sitting in a quiet corner of the mess with a hot Milo. He looked up at the TV screen, where Sky News was being broadcast from the U.K. There was nothing of significance to grab his immediate attention, so he just looked aimlessly at the wall instead.

"Go for your run?" asked a female voice from behind him.

Jo pulled the chair out and sat down opposite him with her own mug of coffee.

"Yeah, it was not bad. Worked up a sweat at least," he replied. "Did you get some sleep?"

The withdrawn look on her face suggested that she hadn't.

"No, not really. I spent some time in the SCIF looking over the SD card and speaking to Canberra."

"And?" asked Kryton.

"Well, mostly there were some contact details on there. I expect it was his case handler's details. Also a few documents written in Russian. NSA is running it through their systems now."

"Fair enough. I suppose we'll just have to wait. What about the forensics?"

After having visited the apartment in Munich, Brenninger had allowed them to view some of the forensic evidence taken from the crime scene. There wasn't too much of significance, however the autopsy had pulled three crushed bullets from the body.

"The Germans will conduct their analysis. Of interest to us will be the calibre of the rounds and make of the weapon. It might not tell us anything, but you never know," explained Jo.

She took a sip from her mug and exhaled deeply. She also knew that if the exploitation of the SD card yielded nothing, then there were no more leads. The CIA were looking for the other scientists, but so far it seemed they weren't having any luck either.

Kryton looked back up at the TV. The coverage was now of the ongoing situation in the Ukraine after the Russian invasion. He smiled when he saw footage of Ukrainian soldiers driving towards the front in Bushmaster Protected Mobility Vehicles that had been donated by the Australian Government. He knew they were great bits of kit, but seeing them only served to remind him of the IED explosion in Afghanistan that had ultimately cut short his army career. Nonetheless, he was perpetually grateful that the Australian designed and manufactured vehicle had saved his life, if not that of his best mate.

"You okay?" asked Jo, bringing him back into the present.

"Umm…yeah. Just thinking about the situation," he replied.

She nodded at him and continued drinking her coffee.

Ten minutes later, they were joined by Cav and Dalton. Both of the operators sat down with a tray full of food, seemingly none the worse for wear from their night on the cans with the AusAID girls.

Cav looked down at his English breakfast in anticipation as he removed the knife and fork from its tightly wrapped serviette. He was about to take a bite of his bacon when he looked at Jo, who was looking at him judgementally.

"What?" he said, before scoffing down the first bite.

She just chuckled and shook her head. Dalton laughed as he poked Cav in the ribs with his elbow, before starting to devour his own breakfast.

9

The Greyfin field operatives once again entered the SCIF to be briefed on the next phase of their ongoing mission. The men looked mostly fresh, despite the efforts of Cav and Dalton to drink the night away. Kryton felt super energetic after his morning run, and was ready to see what Jonas had in store for them.

It was Jo who looked like she was suffering insomnia. She yawned deeply, which didn't go unnoticed by Kryton.

"Make sure you get some sleep after this," he said to her sympathetically.

She nodded in appreciation as she brought her hand across her mouth. She sat down and pulled her fold out chair closer to the wooden table. She proceeded to open a laptop computer and pressed a few buttons, fiddling with the wires at the rear as she did so. A grainy image appeared on the screen. Jo fiddled a little more with the wires and tapped a few buttons.

"Solar flares?" suggested Dalton.

"What!?" mumbled Jo as she looked at the American with an unamused look on her face.

"Well, you never know," replied Dalton with hurt feelings, indicating his question was actually genuine.

"*I* don't think you're stupid," laughed Cav as he patted his colleague on the knee to reassure the big man.

"Okay, cut it out," said Kryton firmly as Jonas' image appeared on the screen.

The three men sat upright as they switched their professional personas back on.

"Morning team, hope you're feeling well rested," said Jonas cheerfully.

46

The team could sense that he had some news.

"What have you guys found?" asked Kryton, seeking to cut to the chase.

"The details you sent were great. This guy logged every detail of his time in protection. Mainly just a journal of his daily activities, but also the details of some of his contacts. We've pulled off numerous selectors which our analysts are running through the systems now."

Kryton smiled and looked at Jo, nodding at her in acknowledgement of her good work to help them get to this point.

"Anything of relevance so far?" she asked Jonas.

"I'll hand over to the lead SIGINT analyst to talk to that," he said, shifting in his seat to allow a young, female uniformed USAF airwoman to sit down next to him.

"Morning sirs, ma'am. I'm Staff Sergeant Luisa Rodriguez on secondment from NSA," said the air force NCO politely. "We've pulled a few selectors from the data provided from your search in Germany. It's actually very interesting."

Selectors are an identifier used in digital communications, such as a telephone number, an email address, or a phone handset. They are a goldmine for SIGINT analysts because, if properly exploited, they can lead to all sorts of intelligence, such as who someone has been talking to or been in contact with electronically.

"What's the main points you can tell us, Luisa?" asked Kryton, leaning into the table.

Rodriguez shuffled through some notes. Like Jo, she tried to stifle yawns that suggested she also hadn't slept in a while.

"Firstly, it seems that Mister Smirnov kept a very basic life. He taught regularly at the local community college in Munich; he contacted his CIA handler on the agreed upon timings; he frequented some local beer halls and restaurants. But apart from that, there is no mention of anything that might suggest a connection to his assassin."

"Jonas, were the scientists directed to keep a journal like that?" asked Kryton.

Jonas shook his head.

"No. It's obviously something he felt the need to do. They weren't issued with anything technical like that SD card. Jo will RV with one of the ASIS guys who will take it by safe-hand direct to an NSA liaison. They will conduct a more thorough extraction of the data, as well as look at the card proper. We might get something from that."

"Sounds fair," said Kryton.

"But that's not the best part," added Jonas. "Luisa, can you continue please?"

"Of course. Umm...the most interesting point is the selectors themselves. We've discovered that one of them is a phone that's been linked to a tower in remote Western Australia, whilst another is linked to a phone located in Munich," she briefed.

"And they've been talking to each other," added Jonas with a knowing look on his face.

"Western Australia?" exclaimed Jo curiously.

She and Kryton looked at each other for a moment, until the light bulb almost went off simultaneously.

"No fucking way," said Kryton, leaning back into his chair and folding his arms behind his head.

"I'm afraid so," said Jonas.

Cav and Dalton looked at each other in a confused manner.

"Want to let us in on it?" demanded the Australian commando.

Jo turned slightly to look at the two shooters.

"Volkov and Smirnov. The two Russians," she said, hoping they would work it out themselves.

"And?" said Dalton, like a dog getting frustrated at its owner for not just giving it the treat.

"Two phones, connected to two locations where two Russians were both assassinated," she added, like an indignant smart girl in high school being forced to tutor the football jocks.

Cav started laughing. He leaned in and spoke softly to his colleague.

"The Russians who were supposed to be oblivious to each other's new whereabouts have been speaking to each other on the telephone."

A look of realisation and relief swept over Dalton's face.

"Urghh...why can't you intel nerds just speak normally?" he said exasperatedly, waving his hands in the air.

"Yes, they have been," said Jonas. "And now that we're all on the same page, we need to look at the 'so what'."

The 'so what' – two little words that intelligence analysts used as the driving force behind all of their work. It was one thing to have information, but it meant nothing unless you then did something with it.

Essentially, it's a way of saying 'what does the information tell us?'; 'what does that mean to us as intelligence professionals?'; and, 'what opportunities are now presented from us knowing that information?'

"What have you guys come up with back there?" asked Kryton, knowing that any analyst worth their salt would already have jotted some thoughts down upon learning this new and intriguing piece of the unfolding puzzle.

Luisa was quick to respond.

"Probably the main point – the one that's actually caused us to breathe a sigh of relief – is that it's now possible that the details of their location and new identities were not found by a system hack."

"Can you be sure of that?" asked Kryton, seemingly not convinced. "What's your evidence?"

"Our evidence is our lack of evidence," responded Jonas. "Neither the CIA or NSA can find anything to demonstrate a breach of the data. Nor can our agencies in Canberra. If the system was hacked and the identities compromised, we'd know about it by now."

Kryton raised his eyebrows and ran his bottom lip across his teeth. Jo knew him well enough to know that that meant he was rapidly processing multiple scenarios in his head.

"Right. So if they were able to talk to each other, they would have had to agree to a communications plan before they were sent off to different parts of the world. Luisa, have any of those other selectors come up with anything else linked to data from on the SD card?"

"Yes, I was just about to get to that. That's the bit making us still feel uneasy. It's actually what we think might be our next lead," said the young USAF analyst as she once again reviewed her notes. "One of the numbers listed on the SD card we have now tracked to a handset in Beirut. It last made contact to a Russian based number three days ago. We're tracking that other connection, and found that it has previously contacted handsets inside Australia, as well as another handset in a general area near Smirnov's apartment in Munich."

"Beirut is where the CIA placed the third scientist," added Jonas, tapping a few keystrokes on his computer in Australia. "He spoke Arabic and had a maternal relative originally from Lebanon, so he was a natural to blend in."

A briefing file appeared on the screen in the SCIF in AMAB. The team observed it closely.

"Aleksei Popov, AKA Aleksei Khoury. Accomplished nuclear scientist; fifty-one years of age; and, like Smirnov, no close family connections in Russia, apart from a distant Uncle who lives in Siberia or something. Certainly nothing that could be used to blackmail him."

"He does look like he has Arab blood, but why did they keep his Russian first name?" asked Dalton.

"Plenty of Russians live in that part of the world, and Aleksei is a common name. The other scientists were given completely different names as it was more conducive for hiding them," said Jonas.

Dalton nodded in understanding.

"So, you're saying that these scientists are not only talking to each other, but also to Russia?" asked Jo.

"That is our initial assessment," said Staff Sergeant Rodriguez bluntly.

"Umm...I want to stress that we're not jumping to conclusions just yet. We want to do more of a deep dive before we brief anything higher. The team are building a strong network chart now," added Jonas.

"I appreciate that you have to play the political game whilst giving your briefings to the bosses, but I'm sure we're all on the same page in thinking what – or should I say who – these guys really are," said Kryton.

Cav leaned across to Jo's chair to whisper in a quiet voice.

"Who?"

She tilted her head slightly to whisper back.

"Sleeper agents."

Holy Shit, mouthed Cav as he leaned back and looked at Dalton.

They didn't need to be rocket scientists in order to appreciate the situation.

"It's a possibility, but far from a certainty. It could be that they didn't fully trust the Americans, and wanted a Plan B in case they had a change of heart. Perhaps they just wanted to keep in touch with each other. Imagine yourself in their shoes. They betrayed their country, and in doing so were shipped off to a foreign land only to be perpetually looking over their shoulders. It would have felt very lonely. Maintaining contact, albeit limited, could have been a means of early warning to the others if something happened to one of them."

"Perhaps," conceded Kryton. "Did you see a phone in the forensic bags we saw with Brenninger?" he then asked Jo.

She shook her head.

"The assassin might have taken it," he mused, before looking back to the screen. "Have you been able to track that handset? The one from Munich I mean."

"We've seen a few pings, but the associated number hasn't made contact to anyone. It's obviously still on, though, as it's being picked up as it passes various phone towers," responded Jonas.

"Where?"

"Umm...yeah, the Middle East," replied Rodriguez, flipping through her notes. "We need more time to narrow it down."

"Near Beirut, per chance?"

"Within a couple of hundred miles."

Kryton smiled and looked at Jo.

"He's going after his next target."

"That's what we think, too," said Jonas. "Problem is, another CIA SAD team was sent to recover Popov from his new home."

"And?" asked Kryton. "No wait, let me guess – he's not there."

"That's correct. His CIA handler has said that he's missed one of their comms windows, but only by a few days."

"Do you think he's gone into hiding? Perhaps if the scientists had their own routine comms windows that were missed, then their SOP was to bolt for it," suggested Kryton.

"That's possible, and that's why this selector is still our best lead," said Rodriguez.

"Perhaps he just went on a holiday and forgot about making contact with his handler?" suggested Cav. "Surely they would have been allowed to lead some sort of normal life, even while in hiding."

"Makes sense," said Dalton. "I've worked on jobs supporting the CIA where they try to teach their assets tradecraft. They don't always adhere to it."

Jonas decided to get on with the next tasking, as discussing the multiple possibilities could go way down a rabbit-hole they simply didn't have time for.

"Alright, let's focus. You're to go to Beirut and await further instructions while we continue to try to locate Popov. We want to be ready to go at a moments notice if that selector pings again."

Kryton looked at Jo with a look of trepidation.

"Beirut? Shit," he mumbled.

Jonas continued giving his instructions.

"If your theory about them being sleeper agents is correct, then there is a third player in all of this, not just us and whoever is killing these scientists. We have to find them – and quickly – to see what their objective is. We're looking at all the options here, based on this new information, to try to make a determination about who the assassin – or assassins – could be. If we hear anything that gets us back onto Boyd, we'll let you know."

51

"And we'll do the same," said Kryton.

Jonas nodded and terminated the connection. His team would not waste a moment trying to join all the dots that would come from their analysis. They would then have to turn it all into actionable intelligence that the Greyfin field team could utilise.

Kryton and Jo looked at each other again. They could only hope that the analysts would come up with something quickly. Neither of them cherished the thought of hanging around waiting for something useful to work with.

And especially not in Beirut.

10

The Greyfin team had been quick to pack up their gear and take a chartered flight to Beirut. The Australian men in the team in particular were still revelling in the novelty of having what did actually appear to be unlimited assets at their disposal. For Dalton, it was just another day in the most well-funded and resourced military on the planet.

Now sitting in the CIA annex at the American embassy in the relatively safe northern suburbs of the capital, they were waiting for the next order in their attempt to retrieve one of the group of scientists that were seemingly being picked off with impunity by a still unknown entity.

The CIA SAD team that had initially been unable to locate Popov had been required for other work, so the Greyfin team had been tasked to take up the search instead.

Kryton sat down in the corner of the small kitchenette where Jo was tapping on her laptop. He passed her a bottle of water.

"Thanks," she said, without lifting her eyes off of the screen.

"Seems like you're always on that thing," observed Kryton playfully.

"Just writing an update report," she replied dismissively, still tapping away while remaining focused on the screen.

"Oh," replied Kryton, taking a sip of water from his own bottle, feeling ignored.

Jo stopped working and looked up at him. He was just sitting there looking at his thumbs, and then looked at her like an ignored child. She rolled her eyes and chuckled.

"Well, are *you* going to write it?" she asked, "or will they?" she then added, motioning to Cav and Dalton who were playing a jovial game of cards on the adjacent table with two of the resident members of the annex.

"No. No I suppose you're right," replied Kryton.

"Well, there you go," she said, winking at him and returning her gaze to the screen.

He smiled, realising that he was a grown man who could find other ways to keep himself entertained. They had been in location for almost twelve hours, and the fact was they had no idea how long they would be there for. They were there based on an intelligence assessment that the assassin might be trying to also locate the next Russian scientist.

But even the Americans hadn't been able to locate him yet. They had utilised local assets to set-up a surveillance operation on his apartment, but so far there had been no further sighting.

They would just have to wait.

******

Several hours later, a gentle shake on his ankle woke Kryton from his sleeping position on the couch in the corner of the recreation room. He looked up to see a young, male CIA analyst looking down at him from the other end of the couch.

"Sir, there's a call for you on the satellite phone."

"Right," said Kryton as he wiped his eyes. "Lead the way."

He jumped up from the couch and followed the young man to the SCIF. It was mostly empty except for two case officers – a middle-aged man, and a young woman – who were sitting together in front of a computer writing a report of their own.

"Here, sir," said the analyst, pointing to a phone on the desk. "Thanks," said Kryton as he picked up the handset of the top-secret, encrypted device and placed it against his ear.

"Kryton here."

"Mate, it's Jonas. We're a go," came the voice on the other end.

Kryton spun around to get the attention of the young man, clicking his fingers as he continued to listen to Jonas.

"Grab the team, please mate," he said sharply in a hushed voice.

The man nodded and continued out of the SCIF.

Kryton pulled a pen from his shirt pocket and started scribbling notes down.

"Yeah…right…understood," he said as he listened to Jonas give his brief.

He furiously wrote down notes, placing the pen between his teeth as he pulled a map out of a drawer and ran his finger across it.

"Rightio. I'll brief the team and we'll get on the road. I'll be in touch," he said, concluding the phone call.

Less than ten minutes later, the Greyfin team assembled in the SCIF and huddled around a table with a map of Beirut spread out on it. A couple of CIA analysts assigned to support the mission were also present. A light flickered on the roof – a consequence of the intermittent electricity supply that the Lebanese capital often suffered from during the middle of the afternoon. Kryton didn't waste a moment in getting into the briefing to the team.

"Okay, signals analysis indicates that Popov – or at least his last known handset – is active in the capital."

He pulled a pen from his top pocket and pointed to the map.

"We've got activity here in the Dekwaneh area. NSA has triangulated the handset to an area the size of several city blocks."

The team studied the map, as well as several corresponding photos of the area hastily produced by the station's analysts.

"That's pretty dense. Reminds me of Ramadi," stated Dalton.

"It is dense, indeed," continued Kryton. "We're going to have to try and reduce the size of the handset's signature, and aim to lock onto whoever has it. Hopefully, it's Popov."

"We'll need more than just us three," said Cav.

"We're four from us, actually. Jo will be coming. We're also taking the two tech guys sitting over your shoulder. This is Paul and Aaron; they're qualified field agents and will have the portable intercept kits that will allow us to narrow the possible location."

"What's the break-up, then?" asked Jo.

"Jo and myself will be in one car. Cav and Dalton, you'll be the snatch and grab team along with…what's his name, the local asset?"

"Ahmed. He's been a long-term asset for us and has the equivalent of a top-secret clearance. He knows everyone – and I mean everyone – in this city. He's one of several assets currently trying to help locate Popov through local networks," said Paul.

"Okay, Ahmed is with you two then."

Cav and Dalton nodded in acknowledgement.

"And Paul and Aaron will be the third team," said Kryton. "We still want to keep this low profile."

"Our primary tasking?" asked Cav.

"Simple – Find; Fix; Finish."

"Finish!?" exclaimed Cav.

55

"Oh…no, sorry. Just playing on words from the old days," said Kryton, realising that the task verb 'Finish' typically meant a less than happy ending for the intended target.

"This is a capture, *not* kill mission," clarified Kryton. "We want this guy alive for questioning."

The team spent the next twenty minutes quickly planning for the task. They knew that whilst the busy traffic of a Beirut afternoon would easily allow them to blend in to the environment, it would also have the opposite effect of making it hard to pick out a person from the crowd. They had an image of Popov to utilise, but that was now several years old, and he could have easily changed his appearance in that time. Additionally, it was possible that the handset they were chasing had been stolen and was being utilised by some petty criminal.

If that was true, then the thief would be about to experience the shock of a lifetime, as the plan called for detaining whoever was found to possess the handset – using any means necessary.

******

A little under two hours later, the full team, divided across three different vehicles, were experiencing the cacophony that was afternoon traffic in downtown Beirut. The CIA station had provided the most mundane and inconspicuous vehicles they could find, which would allow them to blend in with the local environment.

Kryton and Jo sat in a small, red Kia, whilst the American field techs drove parallel to their position several blocks away in an earlier version, albeit silver/grey. Cav and Dalton huddled into the front seat of a Ford Transit minivan with Ahmed, the CIA's local asset in town.

"Anything come up?" asked Kryton frustratedly.

He wasn't the only one getting annoyed with burning petrol whilst covering half of the Lebanese capital during peak hour traffic. The handset had continued to pop up only intermittently, and it was seemingly going from one place to another in unbelievably short periods of time.

"Negative. Still working on triangulating the pings," replied Aaron eventually.

"It's almost as if it's attached to a bird," said Jo.

Kryton just shrugged his shoulders as they sat at yet another red light. Signals and electronics emissions were invaluable for locating and tracking persons of interest for the intelligence agencies using highly sophisticated hardware. Coalition special forces task groups had leveraged heavily on it for targeting operations in both Iraq and Afghanistan. However, like all modern technology, it could often let you down when you needed it most.

Another hour passed.

The intermittent pings of the handset were sufficient to keep the team in the field. They were all experienced in following potential leads to a dead end, so whilst there was still a potential opportunity, they would continue pursuing it until it was proven otherwise. Kryton continued to maintain overall control of the team, and monitored their positions on a small, GPS linked encrypted tablet. Just as it appeared to be a futile effort, an American accent came across the radio.

"Standby for possible target location. Confidence is high," said Aaron.

"About time," said Dalton from inside the minivan as its occupants sat a little more upright, shaking off the stupor that had settled in over the past few hours of aimless wandering.

"Okay, we have a steady signal emission. Confidence is high. Recommend you move to identify target," said Aaron.

Each of the vehicles had been fitted with a repeater device that was programmed to detect the signal and relay it back to the portable intercept kit being operated by the field techs. The vehicles had been moving in what was essentially a triangle format, aiming to box in the signal and make that box smaller and smaller with each ping.

Now, it had finally got to a point where it was possible to start looking for a visual on the handset's location – and on whoever was holding it.

11

The Greyfin team was slowly honing in on their target. The signals intelligence suggested that Popov *could* be nearby, but until they had a firm visual sighting, they would have to assume that it could be anything. Paul focused intently on the screen of the tablet in his lap, and the small pulsating dot that hadn't moved over the past few minutes.

"Possible target in the market place. It's currently static," he said to the team over the radio.

"Roger. Okay, let's go to foot. Cav, I want you out with me to help identify."

"Acknowledged," replied Cav.

The Australian commando fiddled with his own tablet. It had the blue force tracker showing the position of all the teams' vehicles, as well as the target.

"Clay, we're going to have to zip down a few of these smaller streets. Zach's about a street away from the target," he said to Dalton.

The frogman acknowledged, taking a left turn and moving their minivan down a side road of the densely built city. Kryton made a quick assessment of the map, before determining the best position to be dropped off to continue on foot. He directed Jo to a street corner where she could easily pull in and quickly let him out.

"Kryton's on foot," he said discreetly into his concealed radio.

The setting sun ensured that most of the street was in the shade. The afternoon crowd was busy, but not so much that he struggled to move around. He moved through what appeared to be a shopping mall, before coming out to the street on the other side. He already knew what he was looking for: a café nestled between a phone store and a scooter repair shop.

"Send target location," he said.

58

"No change," came the reply from the field tech.

Kryton found a spot by the wall between two shops which allowed him to look across the road. People were settling into the alfresco restaurants, hookah bars, and cafes that ran along the street. An elderly lady stopped and held up a bunch of figs in front of him, trying to sell the small fruit popular in the Middle East.

"La, la," he said, politely declining her with his limited knowledge of Arabic.

The lady simply moved on to the next potential customer, none the wiser to who the large man standing on the wall actually was. A moment later, a familiar voice came across the net.

"This is Cav; I'm at a street corner diagonally across the road from you, Zach."

Kryton took a nonchalant step forward and looked forty-five degrees to his left. Between the rows of moving heads, he could see Cav – and his bushy beard – staring back at him.

"I've got you, mate," replied Kryton, giving a small yet inconspicuous nod.

Cav moved along the street a little closer to the café where the ping was emanating from.

"What's the plan, boss?" he asked.

"I see a spare table out front. Grab it and face the entrance."

"Roger," he replied, turning to walk towards the café.

Less than thirty seconds later, Cav had made it to the front of the café. As directed, he took a seat at an empty table, facing towards the entrance. Once he could see Cav seated, Kryton moved away from the wall and slowly walked across the road. He walked past where Cav was sitting and stood at the entrance of the café. A tinted fly curtain was preventing him from being able to see inside.

He would be entering blind.

Kryton brushed his hand through the curtain and entered the café. He was greeted by loud Arabic music and a café much large inside than he would have guessed from the size of the front exterior. He stood to the side and quickly looked across the several tables, not spending too observing them long lest he look out of place.

"Kryton is inside," he heard Cav say through his ear pierce, relaying the actions to the rest of the team.

"Target is still pinging. In fact, we're picking up a call. Look for someone using a phone," said Aaron.

Kryton went to the counter. The attractive, young waitress greeted him. Assuming the European looking man didn't speak the local language, she spoke to him in English.

"Hello, sir. What would you like?"

"Umm...two coffees. Black, please," he replied, smiling.

He turned to face the interior again to have a closer look at the tables, specifically the customers sitting at them. Typically for the Middle East, half of the people inside were on their phone.

He turned and stepped towards a table by the wall, picking up one of several magazines on top of it. He flicked through several pages as he looked down at what appeared to be a tourist magazine.

"Can you narrow down the location? This place is packed," he whispered into his concealed mic.

Aaron fiddled with a few buttons on his tablet, trying to hone in on the signal to a point that might tell Kryton which seat the handset was located in. Unfortunately, they were not close enough to narrow it down any closer than a ten-metre radius. That covered the entire café. Kryton would have to find out for himself. He turned back to the waitress.

"Do you have a bathroom in here, please?" he asked.

She pointed to the other side of the café at a small hallway leading to its rear. He nodded and smiled, then moved towards it. He deliberately took the longest way possible; slow enough to get a fleeting glance at most of the faces, but not so slow that it would look odd.

As he reached the hallway, he noticed a man sitting alone in a booth facing away from the entrance. He strained at his peripheral vision, trying not to overtly look at the man sipping from a cup ninety-degrees from him. He couldn't quite be sure if that was the phone.

The Australian meandered through the hallway and to the rear of the café. He passed the small kitchen and a storeroom, observing several staff members busily toiling away. He then located the male bathroom, stepping inside and taking a position at the trough. He breathed a loud sigh of relief as he emptied his bladder after several hours of being couped up in the vehicle with Jo. He quickly checked to ensure he was alone in the small room, before speaking again into his mic.

"Nothing seen so far. Cav, I'm going to come back out to you."

"Roger," came the brief reply.

Kryton adjusted his clothes as he finished his business. He quickly washed some water over his face, trying to think of his options. The best idea that immediately presented itself would be to try and initiate a call to the handset and see who in the café picked up at the same time. It wasn't the perfect solution, but it was at least something.

He decided that he would try to find a seat as close to the corner of the café as possible and call Cav in to help him. He left the bathroom and headed back up the hallway towards the main area of the now bustling café.

Although the hallway was only about seven or eight metres long, it afforded him ample opportunity to better view the lone man sitting in the booth that he hadn't quite been able to see previously. Although the man appeared rather gaunt and older than the photo had suggested, it was very clear to Kryton who it was.

Popov.

Well, that was easier than I thought, Kryton thought to himself.

He casually walked past the Russian scientist, deliberately avoiding direct eye contact, but looking close enough to feel positive that it was indeed their target. He continued back to the counter where the two coffees were waiting for him. He thanked the waitress and moved outside, sitting down next to Cav and placing one of the coffees in front of his mate.

"He's inside at the far-right, rear corner," he said, placing the cup to his lips, and sufficiently loud enough to share the details over the radio net to the remainder of the team.

"Roger. I'll relay back to HQ," said Jo.

Cav directed Dalton and his CIA asset partner to move to a location at one end of the street, whilst sending Jo to the other. He quickly discussed with Cav how they might best conduct the snatch. It didn't have to be a spectacular mid-street push into a van like in the movies; it could simply be a case of going up to him in a quiet area, gently placing a pistol into his guts, and telling him to get inside the van which they would arrange to conveniently arrive close enough at just the right time. They were in a foreign environment that they didn't have control of, so they would have to improvise, adapt, and overcome.

That was their remit, though, and they would make it work.

Kryton had observed that there was no observable exit to the rear of the café, and it appeared that Popov was just going through the routine motions of an evening coffee.

Kryton and Cav blended amongst the locals as the street lights and music provided an ambience to the early evening. Kryton took a moment to consider that the lively city – the scene of so much tragedy – would be a nice place to visit in any other circumstances.

He faced away from the entrance, allowing Cav to view the doorway. At any other time, they would likely want to be seated closer to him to observe his actions, and to see who he might be talking to. But this mission was different. It wasn't to watch him; it was to detain him. They would patiently wait for Popov to leave, and look for the opportune time to grab him.

"Aaron, do you have any fidelity on who he was talking to?" Kryton asked.

Any opportunity to gather more intelligence was a good one.

"Negative. We'll have to send the selector details back to NSA to identify that. We haven't got the Gucci kit out here with us today," replied the field tech.

Kryton and Cav both smiled. They appreciated the American's humour. Most of the signals analysts they had worked with, although very smart, could often be somewhat stodgy, so they appreciated a moment of levity during what was, in all reality, a highly illegal operation.

Several minutes passed as the two Australians drank their coffee. Multiple people entered and departed the café, but not the one person they were waiting for. Cav had a limited view inside through a dirty window, but it was hard to tell what movements were occurring inside. The field tech team would be able to advise of any movement, but it was more likely that Cav would see him first.

A few more minutes passed. There was no rush; in fact, the night time would be more conducive for their op. Whilst the main thoroughfares were well lit, the side streets and alleys were less illuminated. That would work in their favour should Popov walk up one of them.

They knew where Popov lived; after all, it was the CIA who had provided it for him, and it seemed that perhaps he had simply just gone away for a few days or weeks, considering that he was now back in town. But the situation had now changed. Someone was out killing the scientists, and there was the additional risk that the scientists themselves weren't all that they had made themselves out to be. Simply going up to him and asking him to come for a chat might allow him to become relaxed, and prevent him from feeling the fear and confusion that a sudden and violent assault would provide. It was hoped that, if he was playing for the other side, the shock of capture was cause him to spill his secrets.

It was getting close to half-an-hour of waiting. The field techs kept sending updates. No change to his location.

"Another coffee?" asked Cav.

Kryton nodded.

"Might as well. Who knows how long we'll be here."

Cav stood up and moved through to the door. As fate would inevitably have it, the one person coming out the other way was the one person they had been waiting for.

"Oh, excuse me," said Cav as he bumped Popov's shoulder.

The wiry Russian looked at the intimidating Australian briefly, before quickly adjusting the glasses on the bridge of his nose, mumbling something incoherent, then walking off. Committed to his cover action, Cav continued on inside, grabbing some serviettes off of the counter.

"He just walked straight past me," he said softly into his mic with a sense of urgency.

Kryton looked over his right shoulder, and then his left.

"Shit," he mumbled to himself. "Jo, he should be coming straight for you."

Jo, having found herself a quiet seat in another café further up the street, was perfectly suited to take up the follow.

"Roger, standby," she said.

Despite their early belief, the Americans had advised the incoming Greyfin team that the Lebanese capital is actually quite safe for solo female travellers, so the attractive, young Aussie spy blended in perfectly amongst the eclectic crowd. She sat adjacent to the direction that Popov would approach from. Despite the increasing number of people out enjoying the evening markets, she was able to spot him as he approached – and then walked past – her location.

"Target now past me and heading south," she said.

"Take up the follow, Jo," instructed Kryton.

She casually stood up and started following him, concealed by the busy evening crowd.

Kryton and Cav, practicing well-rehearsed drills, left the café and split up, with Cav following behind Jo, and Kryton crossing the street to run parallel to Popov's direction of travel.

Further away, Dalton and Ahmed pulled their minivan out into the traffic. They would essentially run zig zag up and down the streets and alleys to ensure that they could pull up alongside and haul the unsuspecting Russian into the minivan once he had been detained. The

American field techs would provide redundancy to assist tracking Popov, just in case the remainder of the team lost visual sighting.

Jo continued to follow Popov, who wasn't exactly setting a cracking pace as he walked along the side of the street past several shops before walking into a market place. It actually made it easier for her to track him, and helped fit her cover of a tourist going for a stroll. Once again the Greyfin team, along with their add-ons, formed a conga line along the streets of an exotic city, following their target. Only this time felt a bit different. They weren't simply following, they were hunting.

Popov wasn't a target; he was their prey.

The Russian continued south before turning up a side street and beginning to head west. Jo relayed the details as she remained the eye – the surveillance term for the person with the visual sighting of the target.

She was comfortable enough to make the call that she could safely, and without compromise, continue to follow him. Kryton and Cav continued to follow at a reasonable distance behind, but not so far that they wouldn't be able to swap out with her if Popov made any sudden change of course. Their aim was to do nothing to arouse his suspicion, yet be close enough to pounce when the opportunity presented itself.

Popov continued west, remaining on the same side of the road. It appeared he was just going for a casual walk. His pace remained slow and steady, and he stopped only occasionally to look in a shop window, or at one of the market stalls on the side of the road.

Aaron's voice suddenly came across the net.

"We've been advised by station that NSA analysis suggests that a recent phone call the target received originated from near here."

"Say again?" asked Kryton.

"He received a phone call from a location nearby. It only lasted less than ten seconds."

Kryton thought quickly as he kept walking. It wasn't the fact that Popov had taken a call, it was the duration of the call that got his attention.

"Can they confirm if the originator has been in contact with the target's phone previously?"

In their vehicle a few blocks away, Aaron quickly reviewed the very brief summary that the NSA analysts had beamed across encrypted satellite and onto his laptop.

"Umm…yes, it looks like it. It'll take them longer to analyse the specifics, but the handset that we're tracking on his possession right now

64

is the same one that had made contact with another handset which is in the area that he's walking to right now."

He's heading to a meet? Kryton thought to himself.

"All callsigns; it's probable that the target is heading to a meeting with someone. We're going to have to grab him before it happens," he said to everyone across the net. "Cav, we'll get you to swap out with Jo."

"This is Cav; acknowledged. Jo, I'll work my way up to you."

"Roger. The crowd is getting thicker, I'm starting to lose sight of him. I actually think he might be speeding up," said Jo.

It was obvious from the noise through her radio traffic that there did seem to be a much larger crowd.

"Why would he be doing that?" Dalton said in his vehicle, looking at Ahmed.

The CIA's most trusted local asset could only shrug his shoulders.

"He's still moving west; but you're right, his pace has quickened," said Aaron, tracking the signal from his own vehicle.

Cav also quickened his pace, trying to hustle through the thickening crowd in order to catch up to Jo. It had caught them all by surprise. For some reason, people had started spilling onto the streets like ants out of their underground home just before it rained.

She had again acquired Popov, and was giving target location indications as she continued through the dense city streets and alleys. Kryton and Cav stayed in the follow, but were themselves struggling to keep pace with Jo.

"He's still moving towards the fringe of the district," informed Aaron.

Kryton had to really exert himself to maintain pace, with each sideways or diagonal movement required to get around people causing him to fall further behind.

"What the…" he mumbled to himself, barely able to hear his own thoughts, let alone the radio traffic, over all of the noise.

"Clay, ask Ahmed what the hell is going on," said Kryton.

"Already on it. He's making his calls."

"Roger," replied Kryton.

Jo's comms were becoming more scattered. By now, Kryton and Cav could only hear the odd word.

Kryton decided to RV with Cav. He gradually worked his way across the street, telling Cav to try to get closer to Jo.

"It's a bloody nightmare here, mate," said Cav across the net.

65

The two teams still in vehicles were also struggling to move through the dense traffic.

"C'mon, move," shouted Dalton as he honked on the horn of his minivan, just like every other driver was doing.

He looked for any means to move his heavy vehicle closer to the location of the team, but none seemed forthcoming. He almost hit two angry looking young men, one of whom turned and banged on the bonnet of the minivan whilst yelling something in Arabic, which he could only assume to be a profanity. The man was about to yell something again, until Ahmed leaned out of his window and gave it back as good as they were being given.

The look on the young man's face turned whiter than the vehicle he had almost been hit by, and Dalton could only assume that his passenger had threatened the two lads with something serious.

"Thanks, I owe you one," he said to Ahmed.

The Lebanese man sat forward, looking out through the windscreen. Even he seemed genuinely confused by all of the racket.

"What's it say on that sign they are holding?" asked Dalton, pointing to several people holding up a banner with Arabic scrawl that by design and hasty construction wouldn't look out of place at an Australian Rules football match.

Ahmed squinted to look at it more closely. He mumbled something inaudible under his breath, then quickly dialled his phone. He clearly appeared impatient, as well as a little nervous. He finally got through to his intended recipient, and had what appeared to be a loud and terse discussion in Arabic.

"Zach, we've got something going on here. Ahmed is going off at someone on his phone."

"What is it?" replied Kryton, still struggling through the pedestrian and vehicle traffic.

Dalton turned his head to look at Ahmed, who was still animatedly speaking into his phone. A moment later, he completed the call.

"We can't go down here because there's a protest on at the stadium," said Ahmed.

"Protest? What protest?" asked Dalton.

Ahmed pointed through the windscreen to the sign Dalton had asked about a moment ago.

"The sign – it says *Death to Israel, Death to America*. We can't go down towards there, it's too dangerous now," he said.

"What the...just wait a minute," said Dalton confusedly, before he proceeded to inform Kryton. "Ahmed says there is a protest on near the stadium and we shouldn't go down there."

"Why? Who's down there?" asked Kryton.

Ahmed looked at Dalton blankly.

"Hezbollah."

Kryton stopped in his tracks.

"Oh, fuck," he said plainly. "Cav, did you hear that?"

"Did he say we're walking into a Hezbollah protest?"

Kryton now started running. They had to locate Jo. Kryton knew that any Hezbollah activity was something that they wanted nothing to do with.

Aaron's voice came across the net.

"Okay, so the station has just informed us that the Israeli's conducted a raid in the West Bank this morning. Several Palestinians were killed."

Kryton could only drop his head, dismayed.

Great, that's all we need, he thought to himself.

He thought for a moment as a large hand grabbed his shoulder. He spun around, ready to defend himself if needed. Cav's face appeared in front of his own.

"It's just me, mate," he said, seeing that Kryton was ready to strike.

Kryton let out a quick sigh.

"This is bullshit. Quick, let's stand over here," he said, grabbing Cav by the elbow and quickly moving the two of them into the alcove of a small shop. "Aaron, switch the blue force tracker on. Give me a location of Jo, as well as Popov."

"Copy...wait out," replied the American field tech.

"Jo, do you hear us?" said Kryton into the radio, still trying to raise his colleague.

There was no audible reply, only static. A moment later, Aaron gave the update.

"Her tracker has her on the overpass just east of the stadium. Her radio is still active."

"Roger. I'm moving there with Cav now."

The Australian men started running – as best as they could anyway – through the almost frantic crowd and towards the stadium. The mostly male crowd was loudly chanting something that they couldn't decipher, but it was intimidating, even to the two experienced operators. Fortunately, the flow of the crowd favoured the direction they were moving, so it was merely a case of politely moving people aside as they proceeded towards her last known location.

"Jo? Jo?" Kryton kept calling into his radio.

The other teams also attempted to raise her on their respective radios, but only static came back. Precious minutes passed as Kryton and Cav pushed to where Jo's tracker had last indicated that she was.

"Both the target and Jo haven't moved," indicated Aaron, still tracking both Jo's tracker and Popov's handset.

All that technology meant nothing until they actually had a visual on her. Suddenly, a garbled and terrified voice came across the net, haunting all of those listening in.

"Zach...help...they've killed," came the screams, until a hissing noise was followed by a sudden electronic squelch.

Then silence.

"The tracker's gone offline," exclaimed Aaron.

Kryton looked at Cav. A sinking and nauseating feeling filled the pits of both of their stomachs, until pure anger and adrenalin forced them to keep on going. The dense nature of the buildings and the narrowness of the streets, as well as the crowd, meant that Aaron had to guide Kryton and Cav towards the last known location. A wrong turn up one street delayed them even longer. They quickly regained their bearings and continued on.

Luckily, the direction they needed to go was now away from the crowd, and they finally made the main road near the Bustan High School and quickly headed south. Now sprinting, the two men could see the overpass ahead. They simultaneously drew their concealed pistols as they reached the bottom of the stairs to the overpass. A flickering light at the top of the stairwell presented an eery sight, and the two soldiers ascended the stairs quickly but methodically, each on one side of the stairwell and with their pistols raised, ready to deal with any threats.

They soon reached the top. The flickering light was coming from the middle of the overpass, and it was clear that the fluorescent tube had only recently been knocked off of its hinges, and was loosely dangling towards the tiled floor. Kryton struggled to clearly see past it towards the other end of the overpass, but it was obvious that something was lying prostrate on the ground. They quickly ran towards it, and soon realised what it was.

A body.

"Oh no," said Kryton, with that sinking feeling increasing in his stomach tenfold.

He sprinted towards it with a speed he hadn't mustered in years. Cav struggled to keep up with him. Kryton soon reached the body. The lights at that end weren't working, but even in the dark he could see a pool of blood from a gun wound to the head. He reluctantly leaned down and turned the body over, not wanting to confirm his horrific suspicions. His body buckled as he let out an uncontrolled sigh of relief.

It wasn't Jo.

Cav joined him and leaned down.

"That's Popov!" he exclaimed confusedly.

Kryton released the body and stood up. He and Cav looked around, trying to look for any sign of Jo. They shouted her name.

There was no response.

They ran down the other set of stairs and onto the footpath, and were now on the other side of the main road. They could hear the chanting of the crowd in the distance, and the main throughfare was almost void of vehicular traffic as a result. Kryton ran into the middle of the road and looked desperately up and down in both directions. He couldn't recall the last time he had felt this desperate.

Or this helpless.

A moment later, Cav appeared by his side. He held up two items. The first was a mobile phone handset, which had been deliberately smashed. The second was a radio receiver with a concealed earpiece.

The same type as Kryton and Cav were both wearing.

The same one – indeed, *the* one – that Jo was wearing.

Kryton ran his hand across his sweaty head. His face turned a pale white as the blood ran screaming into his internal organs to try and prevent his body from going into shock.

"Fuuuck," he yelled, losing his composure for a moment.

He didn't have time to be angry, however. He had to think smart, and act smart. He stood up.

"All callsigns; Guardrail; Guardrail. I say again; Guardrail," he said firmly into the radio to the rest of the team.

A little under three minutes later, a white Ford transit minivan came screeching up next to Kryton and Cav, followed a few moments later by the Kia being driven by Aaron and Paul.

Dalton jumped out of the van.

"Are you sure? Let's look around, she has to be here somewhere," he pleaded.

Cav raised his hand to try to calm the SEAL.

"No mate, it's true," he said, showing Dalton Jo's comms gear, which had clearly been interfered with. "We've looked around. She's gone."

Dalton's jaw dropped. He mumbled something inaudible before quickly kicking into action and jumping back into the van, making comms with the CIA station back at the embassy.

Within five minutes, they had in turn made contact with Greyfin HQ in Australia.

12

The shrill piercing noise of the mobile phone woke Jonas from his deep REM sleep. His first instinct was to attack his clock radio, but when the snooze button failed to stop the incessant noise, his mind cleared enough to look elsewhere for the source of the disruption to his slumber.

He had only put his head down a few hours earlier, having decided against heading home to his inner-Canberra apartment, and instead opting to sleep on an army stretcher in what was once a broom closet. A moment later, several loud knocks rattled the door of the small room.

"Yeah?" he said as he sat upright.

"Sir, you're wanted immediately in the JOR," came the voice of the overnight watchkeeper from the other side of the door.

"Hmm…yeah, okay. I'm coming," he replied.

He finally grabbed the phone from beside the stretcher and looked at the screen. The three letters *JOR* appeared. He quickly pressed the button to answer the call.

"I'm coming," he said sharply, not even waiting for a reply.

He stood up and placed some clothes on, then quickly went to the bathroom and splashed some water on his face. He looked at his watch. *0430.*

Now alert, his mind started to wonder what the wake-up call might be about. He walked the thirty or so metres to the JOR, swiped his access card, and walked through.

A young RAAF airman was holding a phone receiver in his hand, looking at him worryingly. Jonas then actually noticed the colour of the phone. It wasn't any phone the airman was holding; it was the red phone that provided the emergency line to CIA headquarters at Langley.

Fuck, thought Jonas as he sprinted the last few paces to the desk.

"This is Jonas."

71

He listened intently for a few moments. His knees almost buckled at what came across the line. His mouth hanging agape caught the attention of the airman who had resumed his seat in the watchkeeper's desk.

Jonas hastily motioned for him to fetch a pen and paper. The airman hesitated for a moment as he glanced around the desk; the digital age meant that such items were less ubiquitous than they once were.

Joans covered the mouthpiece and clicked his fingers at the airman, pointing to an adjacent desk.

"Over there, for fucks sake…" he whispered impatiently.

The airman retrieved the pen and paper and handed it to Jonas, who proceeded to madly scribble down some notes whilst he continued the conversation.

"Yes…no…roger…have you informed JSOC?…okay, good."

The entire exchange lasted less than a few minutes.

Jonas slammed down the receiver and took a valuable moment to make an appreciation of what was required. He opened a draw under the watch desk and pulled out a red folder, slapping it onto the table and furiously opening the cover before flipping through several pages. By now, the few skeleton staff that comprised the overnight watch were looking at Jonas in curious anticipation.

"Boss…what is it?" asked one of the other uniformed members sitting at a desk.

Jonas looked up as his mind kept racing.

"Right, listen in. Guardrail has been signalled. This is not a drill."

The watch team looked at each other for a moment, before launching themselves back into their desks and onto their computers or phones.

Guardrail – The codename for when a Greyfin member is either kidnapped, captured, or goes missing in the field.

Jonas flipped through a few more pages to find what he was seeking: the standard operating procedures for the steps to take in what had been expected to be – up to this point at least – a highly unlikely scenario. So unlikely that they had practiced the drill only once since the formation of the team, hence the need to pull out the doctrine.

"Okay," commenced Jonas, composing himself, "US team – Langley has informed JSOC and CENTCOM who will go on standby. Get NSA to start focusing on chatter. The CIA will start looking at their regional networks for any HUMINT. Jo's profile is uploaded in the personnel files. Get that to them ASAP."

He turned slightly to look at one of the other watchkeepers.

"Australian team – inform the SOCOMD watchkeepers to get offshore recovery alerted. I'll head around to the JOC JOR and get the ASIS LO in."

He took an additional moment to think. The empty desks in front of him presented the logical next step.

"And get everyone in…now. If it has been a kidnapping, we'll likely find out about it on open-source intelligence channels or, Christ forbid, the media, before we find her through other means."

The watchkeepers didn't need to be told twice. They had been deliberately assigned to the highly classified unit because of their maturity, intellect, and ability to handle a crisis. This one would certainly test every one of those attributes.

Jonas raced out of the sub-basement of the Greyfin JOR and up the narrow tunnel towards the stairs leading up to the main floor of the HQJOC JOR. The large open plan floor housed the nerve centre of all global ADF operations. He swiped his access card and entered. Multiple large screens displayed all sorts of information, such as known locations of military vessels near Australia and in the South China Sea, as well as air movements in the same area. A smaller TV displayed 24/7 news coverage. The lead story was regarding an Israeli attack in the West Bank the day before – as well as the loud, and often violent, protests in the Arab nations that followed.

Jonas raced over to the watchkeeper's desk, asking the on-duty soldier where the watch officer was.

"He's making a coffee, sir," replied the young man, motioning to the corner of the large room where a kitchenette was.

Joans sprinted over to find a middle-aged, slightly larger than the recruiting poster would likely show, navy commander rubbing his eyes and waiting for the kettle to boil. No doubt the naval officer was looking forward to the end of his twelve-hour shift in just over an hour from now. He had no idea that his night was about to take a dramatic turn.

"Mate, we've got an emergency," said Jonas.

The naval officer looked at Jonas and smiled, before returning his attention to the kettle as he poured the hot water into his mug.

"What have you got?" he said, not in a dismissive manner, but certainly without much enthusiasm, and perhaps thinking Jonas was just another Defence Department contractor about to report some IT issue.

Jonas stepped closer and spoke quietly into the ear of the commander.

"I'm up from Greyfin…we're calling Guardrail."

The officer's head snapped up as he looked again at Jonas. The look in the eyes of the man standing mere inches from him simply reinforced what he had just heard.

"Oh, shit," he said, placing the mug down and reaching into the pockets of his navy grey camouflage pants.

The officer fumbled for a moment, struggling to grasp his pen as he opened his notebook. Jonas empathised with him, realising that he probably looked exactly the same only a few minutes earlier when he had been informed by the CIA.

"Do you know the process?" Jonas asked him calmly.

"Yes…we've got the SOPs ready. Who do you want alerted first?"

The considered question gave Jonas confidence that the officer knew how to deal with it without additional supervision.

"I need the ASIS LO in here ASAP. We're speaking to SOCOMD, so let's not double hat that. We're also covering international partners."

The officer made some notes as he walked briskly with Jonas over to his watch desk.

"Oh…you'll have to advise CJOPS," added Jonas.

CJOPS – the Chief of Joint Operations – is the three-star officer who runs HQJOC, and by default manages all ADF operations globally. He would be responsible for informing the politicians that a young, female Australian spy had likely been captured whilst conducting an intelligence operation in a hostile environment on the other side of the world.

13

Kryton paced up and down the outside of the CIA's Beirut SCIF like a caged tiger at a zoo. For the first time in years, he puffed on a cigarette. The bland tobacco taste was awful, but it at very least kept his hands occupied. The light patter of rain echoed off of the tin roof, as the early morning sunshine became obscured by dark clouds.

A most appropriate sentiment for the current situation.

It had been seven hours since Jo had gone missing; kidnapping still being the most likely scenario. The men had stayed out for several hours, trawling every street, alley, and drain around the area where she had been last heard from, but to no avail.

Kryton played those last, haunting words from her radio in his head again and again.

Zach...help.

He couldn't stop thinking about it. He kept asking himself what could have been done differently.

The clanking sound of the heavy SCIF door opening distracted his morbid thoughts for just a moment. Dalton appeared next to him.

"Those things will kill you," he said, trying to ease the tension.

It was no use. Kryton just stared at the ground.

"I did this, Clay," he said softly.

"No, you didn't," said Dalton firmly, trying unsuccessfully to reassure the Australian. "We did it all by the book. There is no way we could have known what was in front of us."

Kryton crushed the remainder of the half-smoked cigarette on the side of the bin and threw it away.

"Maybe; but it was still my op."

The American could see that his colleague – a man who he had grown to admire and trust – was devastated. He also knew, from the little that

Cav had told him, that Kryton still blamed himself for an incident in Afghanistan that had killed his best friend.

"If anything, it's my people's fault. They should have warned us," said Dalton, kindly looking to apportion blame onto his own team.

The reality was, it was simply a few small factors, which combined, had a catastrophic consequence. The two men stood in silence for a moment. The feeling of helplessness was the worst feeling an operator could possibly have. All that training, experience, and skills meant nothing right now. However, the pity party would have to wait. The clanking noise of the SCIF door was followed by Cav sticking his head out.

"They're ready," he said.

Kryton and Dalton walked towards the door and inside to the SCIF. They walked down the hallway and into the crowded audio-visual briefing room. The room was packed. Every analyst assigned to the station was jammed along the back wall. The CIA station chief sat at the head of the desk facing the screen, which itself was jammed with small boxes showing multiple locations dialling into the meeting.

All the key players were in attendance. The Americans were represented by JSOC; NSA; CIA; CENTCOM; as well as the National Security Advisor, who would chair the meeting. On the Australian side was SOCOMD; HQJOC; representatives from the intelligence agencies; as well as Jonas and his team.

Kryton took a seat next to the station chief. He shook his head to wake himself up, suddenly realising that he hadn't slept in close to thirty-six hours. He grabbed a bottle of water from the middle of the large boardroom style desk, opened the lid, and consumed most of it in one gulp. That freshened him up enough to focus on the task in front of them.

"Okay, let's get this started," said James Rand, the U.S. National Security Advisor. "We've got an intelligence operative missing, believed captured, is that correct?"

The way he asked the question led pretty much everyone to think it was rhetorical. It wasn't.

"Is that correct?" he asked again firmly.

The station chief reached over and softly grabbed Kryton's arm.

"This is for you," he whispered.

Kryton looked up at the screen. He hadn't been paying attention, having once again been distracted by his internal thoughts. He looked around the room to find every face looking straight at him. He sat upright, looked at the screen, and cleared his throat.

"Umm…Sergeant Zach Kryton, sir; Greyfin team leader," he commenced, introducing himself for the wider audience. "Yes, that is correct. Our team was conducting an operation against a POI within the Beirut area. The aim of that op was to identify and detain the POI who is suspected of being part of a possible Russian intelligence operation against western interests."

He paused to take another sip of water. He didn't really need the hydration; it was to give himself a moment to gather his thoughts before he continued.

"During that op, sir, at approximately twenty hundred hours Beirut time, Greyfin officer Joanne McKenzie was likely kidnapped or detained by an as yet unknown entity."

Dalton looked at Cav.

"McKenzie!?" he mouthed, suddenly feeling foolish that to that point he hadn't even learnt Jo's surname.

"Assessed?" asked Rand.

"Yes, sir. The last comms we received during the op was a distress call from her. Myself and my team moved rapidly to her last known location near the Beirut stadium. Once there, we found her radio equipment, as well as the body of the POI. He had been shot, and it appeared as if he had been executed."

Rand flipped through a few pages in a file on his desk.

"This POI was the Popov character you were following?" he asked.

"That's correct, sir."

The president's key advisor on national security issues flicked through the file. A former military man himself, he understood that even the most well laid plans get disrupted by factors that are beyond control. He had previously been briefed into the Greyfin project, but wouldn't necessarily be completely over every minuscule detail of their operations.

"Okay. What's your initial assessment, Sergeant?"

"I believe that Jo…err, Miss McKenzie…got caught up in an opportunistic kidnapping by a group of locals involved in the protest resulting from an Israeli strike in the West Bank a day earlier. That would be the most likely scenario," he said succinctly.

The truth was, he really didn't know what to believe. What he had just briefed was indeed the most likely scenario, but he didn't care about the 'why'. He just wanted to get her back.

"It is also the best-case scenario," he had to add.

"The *best*-case scenario?" asked Rand curiously.

Kryton had to think for a moment. The questions being asked were perfectly fair, and required an analytical answer from a trained analyst, which he was. Speaking so bluntly about a close friend in such a manner was difficult for him. It would be difficult for anyone.

"Yes, sir. If that has happened, then either they will let her go once they realise that she isn't an Israeli or an American, or the local police will find her through their networks."

"Mister Mason, is that your assessment?" Rand then asked the station chief.

The obviously tired CIA officer also leaned forward in his chair.

"Well, sir, that is certainly one plausible scenario. It's too early to know more. I have my team scouring every local asset to try to find any piece of information that might give us a lead. They had adequate cover for the operation, so we've also engaged local law enforcement to assist with the search."

Rand looked a little confused as he looked at his own screen.

"If Sergeant Kryton's assessment is accurate, or even close to it, then why have we got special operations on this call?"

Mason shifted in his chair, looking around the room. No one – no one inside the SCIF in Beirut at least – had an immediate answer.

It was an Australian accent that broke the silence.

"Sir, this is Jonas Sherrin, operational manager for Greyfin. Standard operating procedures call for informing special operations in the event of the possible capture of a field agent. The sensitive nature of this work, if compromised, presents a grave national security threat; to both the U.S. and Australia."

Cav leaned in and whispered to Dalton.

"Sherrin!? Once we get through this, we need to get to know the people on this team better," he said, personally disgusted that he was only now learning the surname of a team member for the first time, for the second time in as many minutes.

Dalton nodded in agreement.

Back on the screen, Rand looked at the file as he finished listening to Jonas' explanation, then looked up.

"And that would be in the event of a *worst*-case scenario, I'm guessing?"

"Umm…yes, sir," replied Jonas.

Rand spent the next few minutes getting opinions and options from across the various stakeholders in attendance. The military folk sat quietly whilst the intelligence agencies debated everything that might have influenced a kidnapping – ranging from a simple ransom opportunity, through to terrorism somehow associated with the war in Ukraine.

"Okay, okay, enough," said Rand, holding his hands up to regain control of the conversation. "Mister Sherrin, give me a quick summary of the next course of action."

Jonas looked down at his notebook and composed his response.

"Sir, for now, this is an intelligence effort. The focus will remain on local assets and networks within Lebanon, as well as adjacent countries, to pick up any chatter by whatever means necessary. Once her location and status have been identified, we'll look at options for recovery."

Kryton sat back in his chair and rubbed his hands through his hair. He recalled the exercise only a few weeks earlier on the Gold Coast, where the team had practiced for just this scenario. He couldn't believe they were now in this situation.

He still blamed himself.

A firm grip on his arm disrupted his day dreaming. He looked up and saw the station chief looking at him, motioning towards the screen with his eyes. He quickly glanced around the room and once again saw all sets of eyes on him, and then at the screen to see Rand also waiting for him.

"Well, are you good to lead your team or not?" asked Rand, obviously not for the first time in the last few moments.

Kryton sat upright and nodded his head.

"With everything I've got, sir."

14

Kryton and Dalton thanked the police officer as they departed his small office in the north of Beirut. The police inspector had been sympathetic to their cause: looking for their missing tourist friend who had not been seen since she had gone for an evening walk two nights earlier. He had promised to place the usual alerts, but their focus was on the aftermath of the protests that had occurred in roughly the same area.

"Another dead-end," cursed Kryton as he slammed the passenger door close.

Dalton just fastened his seatbelt, placed their vehicle into gear, and pulled out of the parking lot of the police station. He knew words wouldn't make any difference, so he wouldn't waste them with false optimism. The window traditionally utilised by law enforcement to find a missing person – the famed forty-eight hours – was fast closing, and they appeared no closer to locating Jo.

Kryton looked aimlessly out of the window as Dalton drove through the bustling city streets back towards the embassy. That nauseating feeling in the pit of his stomach was getting worse, and he was certain that he would end up with an ulcer by the end of it. He didn't care. He felt that it was probably the least that he deserved. His mind quickly turned back to that day in Canberra where he had offered her a spot on a new covert operations team that would ostensibly help make the world a lot safer.

Right now, he was wishing that he had never made the offer. As far as he was concerned, the world could go to hell; and he would burn it down if necessary in order to get her back.

The drive back to the embassy took them about twenty minutes. Dalton slowed as he approached the sprawling U.S. diplomatic mission, clearly indicated by the large American flag waving in the breeze coming off of the Mediterranean. The two operators pulled their identification cards out and showed them to the two-armed Marines standing guard at the entrance point.

The ambassador had taken the advice of the station chief and enhanced security – standard procedure for in response for what could be the worst-case scenario that had been discussed a day earlier. Although Jo was an Australian, the nature of the Greyfin project ensured that all members were essentially treated like U.S. nationals, and afforded all rights and privileges to go with it.

"Sir, your presence is requested immediately in the annex," said the large, intimidating guard to Kryton.

Kryton nodded as he took back his card. He looked at Dalton, who just shrugged. The SEAL drove the vehicle into the main compound, continuing up to another gate where plain-clothed guards – all U.S. citizens and most likely former military types – were conducting security for the CIA annex. Once through, they pulled up outside of the SCIF. The two of them got out of their vehicle and were greeted by Cav.

"What's going on?" asked Kryton.

"Some contact called in with a lead, about an hour ago. We've been trying to call you."

Kryton pulled out his phone as he walked to the foyer of the SCIF. The screen indicated several missed calls.

"Shit," he mumbled as he shook his head in frustration.

He was pissed at himself. In his malaise, he was starting to forget some of the basics, such as comms checks. He vowed that that would end right now. He placed his phone in a secured box, and looked up at the two shooters looking at him in a concerned manner. They could sense – and see – his general disquiet. He took a deep breath and stood a little more upright.

"I'm good, boys; seriously."

"Still in the fight?" asked Dalton.

"You bet."

Cav slapped him on the arm and nodded, and then all three of them walked into the SCIF.

Several of the station's analysts, as well as the station chief, once again sat around the long table facing the main screen. An IT technician was establishing the communication bridges. A moment later, they could see Jonas, soon followed by some other people that Kryton didn't quite recognise. He walked over to the Mason, who was madly writing down some scribbles in his notebook.

"Chief; what's happening?"

Mason looked up. His facial expression looked like he had just found his missing car keys.

"Oh, good. You're back. About sixty minutes ago we received word through some intelligence back channels that indicated a possible location for Jo."

"Intelligence back channels?" asked Dalton.

"Once Jo went missing, and along with using our own resources, we placed alerts out to trusted regional partners to seek their assistance finding her location."

"I see," said Dalton.

"You've got something?" asked Kryton, with just a tinge of optimism in his voice – the first such feeling he'd had since she went missing.

"Yes. One of our partner liaison officers has reached out through Langley stating that an asset of theirs – a regional asset – has made contact claiming they know her location."

Kryton looked at Dalton cautiously.

"Confidence level?" he asked Mason.

"Well, that's what you're going to go and find out," replied the station chief.

"Alright; when do we leave?" asked Dalton, jumping the gun.

Kryton put his hand up to get his colleague to ease up on the enthusiasm.

"Hang on; a partner liaison officer? Who is it?"

"It's the Israelis."

Dalton's enthusiasm suddenly dried up.

"Ah, shit," he lamented.

"Problem?" asked Mason.

"No. Well, sort of. We had a bit of a run in with them recently. A few crossed wires," replied Kryton.

"Is that going to be a problem?" asked the station chief.

Kryton shook his head.

"No. We'll go."

Mason motioned for them to follow him over to the desk of one of the analysts. He picked up an A4 file and opened it. A hastily compiled memo had been created detailing the LO's intelligence.

"The Israelis didn't share much. They're a bit old school and they want to meet face-to-face. I don't think they trust the digital age," he briefed.

"Perhaps they don't trust an agency that produced the likes of Edward Snowden," suggested Cav.

It was an off the cuff comment, but one that lacked diplomatic consideration. Kryton gave a displeasing look to his mate. Mason was about to say something, but facts have a way of winning the argument.

"Well, Julian Assange is an Australian, so we're all susceptible to producing traitors," mused Kryton quickly, trying to head off any conflict at the pass.

Mason looked at Kryton, then back at the file. A small smirk appeared in the corner of his mouth.

"Yes, well. Anyway, they are very protective of their sources. You'll have to go and meet them personally and see what they have."

"Who and where?" asked Kryton.

Mason flipped the file around and handed it to Kryton. The three Greyfin operators huddled around it and read the contents. Kryton scrolled down and found what he was fearing.

Person of contact: Jacob Levy.

Cav found the name at the same time, then looked up at Kryton. He was about to say something, but Kryton quietly shook his head to stop him. He didn't think Mason needed to know that they already knew Levy; he was worried that the station chief might not let them go if he thought that there was a risk that the Mossad officer wouldn't speak to the Greyfin team again. Kryton was determined to go to that meet. He would deal with the potential that the Israelis viewed the incident as amateurish later.

"Where is it?" he asked.

"Here, in Beirut. Mossad will send details. I expect it will be sooner rather than later."

Kryton nodded his head.

"Good. We'll go and get prepared, and touch base here again in an hour for further instructions. Can you inform Jonas in Canberra?"

"We're on it," replied Mason.

The three operators left the SCIF and walked back outside. They moved over to the smoking area and stood under the shade of a large fig tree.

"So, Levy *is* Mossad," stated Dalton.

83

"Yeah, but we already knew that. I'm curious as to why he's in Beirut, though," said Kryton.

"Could they be fucking with us? Payback for Dubai, perhaps?" asked Dalton.

Kryton thought about that for a moment, then shrugged his shoulders.

"I have no idea, but we need to exhaust all lines of enquiry."

"If he's a senior Mossad agent, or even just a handler, then he would get around the region quite a bit I would imagine," suggested Cav.

It was a good point. Australians and Americans – as people coming from geographically large countries – could often forget just how close many Middle Eastern nations were in proximity to each other, especially those bordering the Mediterranean. Kryton nodded, then focused on the job ahead, rather than go down the rabbit hole of scenarios and semantics.

"Okay. Usual SOPs for the Op. I'll take the meet; you two are the cover team; usual kit; and, once we find out the location of the meet, we'll do a quick planning session and then execute. Questions?"

Cav and Dalton both smiled.

"What?" asked Kryton.

"Nothing. Just glad to have you back," said Cav.

Kryton lowered his head. He knew that he had been letting his guilt distract his focus. But this was the best lead that they had received so far, and he was determined to make the most of it.

"Let's hope this prick knows where she is," he said.

15

Cav and Dalton slowly worked their way into place on the opposite side of the road from the café where the meeting with Levy was to take place. The Israelis had not wasted any time, and the instructions for the meeting had been received via the CIA just before lunch.

It was expected to be a collegial meeting, but Cav and Dalton carried concealed weapons just in case. After what had happened days before – and the very reason for them having to be there talking to the Israelis again – meant that they would not trust anyone.

The instructions from the Israelis included a pre-arranged phrase to confirm respective identities. Old school tradecraft indeed, but still useful in the modern age. It had given the team the confidence that it was a genuine lead, because if Levy had known it was Kryton who he was meeting, then they wouldn't have provided the requirement for an identification signal.

It appeared that as far as the Israelis were concerned, a Mossad agent had alerted his handler to the whereabouts of a young woman who had been kidnapped, and that it was possible it might be the woman the CIA had lost during a routine operation that had gone wrong.

Kryton sat in a vehicle a block away with his CIA driver, waiting for the call from his cover team. The clock ticked by, and soon it passed the designated time.

Then another five minutes.

Then ten.

"Do you think they're doing the same thing we are?" asked Dalton from his seat in a bar across the road and adjacent to the café.

"They don't know what *we* look like, ostensibly at least," replied Cav.

"Oh, yeah. I forgot," acknowledged the frogman.

"The instructions indicated that he'd be sitting with his legs crossed and having a coffee whilst reading the finance section of today's paper," said Kryton.

"Roger," said Cav.

"Copy that," said Dalton.

"It doesn't matter. We know what *he* looks like…assuming it is Levy who comes," said Kryton.

He looked at his watch. It was almost fifteen minutes after the pre-arranged time. Maybe he was late. Maybe they were doing their own recon before settling in. Kryton hadn't worked with the Israelis before so he didn't know their methodologies.

He made an encrypted call back to the embassy.

"Have you heard anything to suggest they cancelled the meet?" he asked the operational team.

"No, sir. We're still expecting a meet at the designated time and location."

"Roger. Thank you," replied Kryton. "We'll just have to wait, lads," he then informed his team over the radio.

He let out a deep sigh and closed his eyes. It would certainly not be the first time he would have been left hanging by a contact. It happened all the time in Afghanistan. But that was a country with people who measured time in weeks, months, and years, rather than seconds and hours. He expected better from a professional intelligence officer. Perhaps it was just Mossad's way of showing the CIA who was boss in this part of the world. After all, it was an American that Levy was expecting to meet, not an Australian.

His thoughts were disturbed by Dalton's firm voice over the radio.

"I think we have something."

Kryton sat upright in the passenger's seat, listening intently.

He waited for a moment.

And then another.

"What is it?" he asked.

There was no reply.

A loud rattling noise scared the life out of him and his driver. He quickly reached for his pistol, but stopped when he saw Cav standing next to the window. Kryton leaned out to look at the commando.

"He's here. Your radio must be fucked cos I could hear Dalton, but we couldn't hear you."

"Fuck me," said Kryton angrily, ripping the radio from his body and handing it to the driver. "Get this fixed, will you mate? We're going to continue with the meet."

The driver nodded in an unsurprised manner that suggested it wasn't the first time their station-issued technology had failed them during a job. Kryton and Cav set off the two short blocks to the café.

"Actually, you find a spot next to me so you can have comms to Dalton. Which way is Levy facing?"

"Towards the ocean but slightly south. We'll be approaching him from his rear," replied Cav.

"Rightio. I don't want to scare him, but I want to catch him a bit off guard, too."

"That won't help much with rapport," said Cav.

The two men shuffled quickly across the road, narrowly avoiding a distracted taxi driver.

"I couldn't care less about rapport. We get what we came to find, then we get the hell out of here and go and get Jo."

"Roger that," replied Cav.

He knew Kryton well enough that when he had a plan in mind, he was going to stick with it. Thirty seconds later, they rounded the corner and were now in sight of the café. Kryton immediately identified Levy sitting alone at a table, with his legs crossed and reading the finance section of the daily paper. He was certainly looking the part of a local national, dressed in pants and cheap loafers, with a collared button up shirt that was well in need of an iron.

Kryton quickly surveyed the myriad of people milling in the general area. No-one in particular stood out as a threat; not that they were expecting it, however. It would be Dalton's job to provide look-out.

Kryton walked past Levy and softly sat down adjacent to him. The Israeli spy quickly glanced at his new companion through his Ray-Ban sun glasses.

"The economy isn't what it used to be," said Kryton, using the verbal signal agreed upon by the operational teams who facilitated the meeting.

Levy placed the paper down on the table.

"No, but at least the stock market provides opportunities..."

Levy's voice trailed off before he could finish the sentence.

"I know you," he said with some uncertainty.

Kryton took his own Oakley sunglasses off and leaned in a little closer towards Levy. The Israeli, feeling ambushed, quickly turned his head, only to see a large Australian commando sitting in the seat opposite staring deadpan straight back at him.

"What is this?" protested Levy. "I'm not alone."

"Neither are we," retorted Cav aggressively.

Levy stood to leave, but Kryton quickly sought to defuse the situation.

"Mister Levy, please. We need your help. I apologise for my colleague's brashness," he said, holding his hands up in a peaceful gesture.

Cav was probably still bitter at the Israelis because of the fight in the shopping mall in Dubai, but his tone had inadvertently allowed them to play a little 'good cop, bad cop' with Levy.

"Please?" said Kryton again, gesturing for the Israeli to retake his seat.

Levy looked down at Cav, who sat back in his seat submissively, then sat back down and faced Kryton. The Australian knew that rapport would certainly be required now, despite his ill-considered statement to Cav only moments earlier as they approached the meeting.

"I was expecting to meet the Americans," said Levy.

"Well, we're the Americans; for now, at least. I'm Kryton…Zach Kryton," responded the Australian as he leaned in closer to speak softly, deliberately using his full name to try to build some trust, even though he knew that Levy already knew it. "We understand that you might know where one of our people is."

Levy looked at Kryton for a moment to assess the situation. He had no reason to not believe Kryton's affiliation with the CIA. After all, they had met under different circumstances in Dubai, so he knew the Australians were military, and most likely intelligence affiliated. The identification confirmatory phrase had been utilised, so he was confident that these were the people he was there to meet.

"I'm sorry to hear of your predicament," he said to Kryton, suddenly taking a more amicable tone and demeanour.

"Thank you," responded Kryton. "I cannot explain the details behind how this has come to be, but I can tell you that she is an invaluable member of our national security apparatus, and that our operation was not in conflict with your national interests."

Levy just smiled and nodded his head. He knew full well that he wouldn't get all of the details, and that intelligence operations in the region were always undertaken in hostile conditions. It was obvious she was an intelligence officer of some sort. Why else would the CIA be asking of her whereabouts?

"I understand completely, Mister Kryton."

"Okay, then. She has been missing for close to forty-eight hours. We've not heard from her in that time. A large protest occurred near the stadium at the same time. We think that during that protest, she has been kidnapped."

"Oh. I see," replied Levy, perhaps with just a tinge of sympathy and guilt in his voice; after all, the protest was the direct result of the Israeli strike in the West Bank.

"After your American friends reached out to us, we naturally alerted our assets here to try and help find out her location. We got a reasonably quick response that one of our assets might know something that can help you."

"Might?" queried Kryton.

"One of my case officers has already met with the asset. He's on his way here to brief me. You're welcome to stay for that, if you like," said Levy.

Kryton looked at Cav to get his take on this news. He only nodded and shrugged his shoulders in response. Cav's thoughts matched Kryton's own, in that all seemed above board.

"We would appreciate that, if you don't mind?"

"Excellent. Then I will get us some tea. Is that still what the descendants of British settlers still drink?" asked Levy jokingly.

Kryton let out a small laugh; an unconscious reaction that didn't mirror the aching feeling still residing in his stomach. Levy obviously knew some Australian history.

"That would be fine, thanks."

Levy nodded and stood to walk inside the café. Kryton thought for a moment, then realised that Levy reminded him of one of his lecturers from years ago at Adelaide University. Aloof at times; then charmingly charismatic; then serious to the point of scary. One of the key traits that many agencies look for when recruiting their spies is the ability to alter a persona at a heartbeat.

He looked over at Cav.

"Go and check in with Dalton. Four of us here might get a bit crowded."

"Roger. We'll stay within visual range," replied Cav, before getting up and walking across the road.

Kryton exhaled deeply and recapped in his mind the conversation so far.

Please, let him know where she is, he thought to himself.

He watched the people walk past as the afternoon crowd prepared for the evening, and the bars and restaurants would soon be full yet again. He looked at the paper and picked it up, giving the articles a cursory glance without any due consideration. He wasn't the least bit interested in what was going on in the rest of the world. He folded the paper over on itself and placed it down on the table.

"Here you go," said Levy as he returned to the table with a tray holding a teapot and two cups.

He placed the contents onto the table proper before sitting back down. Kryton poured them a cup each, and let the hot drinks settle for a moment.

"Oh, no. We can't have that," said Levy as he picked up the paper and placed it down by his side.

"What is it?" asked Kryton, suddenly alarmed.

Levy smiled, almost embarrassingly.

"Oh, nothing really. The way you folded and placed the paper. It's a signal we use to abort a meeting. My officer might think that I don't want to talk to him."

"Oh, sorry. You mean your *Katsa* might not want to talk to you!" replied Kryton.

Levy looked across the top of the cup he was cooling with his breath and smiled at Kryton. He was impressed.

"Yes…my Katsa. Do you speak Hebrew?" asked Levy, thinking that seeing as the Australian knew the Mossad utilised term for field agent, then he might know more of the language central to Judaism.

"No, I'm afraid that is the limit of my knowledge," replied Kryton.

Levy was quickly warming to the Australian. For the next five minutes, they chatted in general about mindless topics, with both sharing just a little bit about themselves without giving too much away. Cav and Dalton watched from a bar across the road, seated at the bench that looked out across the street.

"You think this guy knows anything?" Dalton asked.

"Buggered if I know, mate. We need to try every avenue, though."

Dalton nodded as he chewed on some more of the complimentary nuts.

The two special forces operators kept a close eye on the small table across the road, watching as another man eventually joined Kryton and Levy. The skinny man with a dark complexion and black framed glasses spent twenty minutes huddled next to Kryton and talking. At one stage, he pulled out some paper and drew on it as he continued speaking to Kryton, who asked questions in return. Levy only spoke occasionally.

"Looks serious," said Dalton.

"Looks positive," replied Cav. "I doubt they would have spoken for this long if he didn't have anything."

Another five minutes passed before Kryton concluded the meeting with Levy and his fellow spy. They all shook hands, before the two parties moved off in opposite directions. Kryton jogged across the road and joined Cav and Dalton.

"So?" asked Cav.

Kryton took a seat next to them and softly laid the piece of paper he had taken notes on down on the bar.

"Well, they've told us one of their agents – who is integrated into Hezbollah – has told them that Jo was indeed taken. The assumption was that she was an Israeli spy."

"Israeli spy?" exclaimed Dalton.

"Well, the fanatic Arabs think every non-Arab is an Israeli spy," explained Kryton. "She was held in one of their safe-houses for about a day to the north of the country. Apparently, some young and enthusiastic punks thought they would gain favour with their leadership by capturing an Israeli spy."

"Oh, shit," mumbled Dalton forlornly.

"Do they know where she is right now?" asked Cav.

"Not exactly," replied Kryton, only to be met with confused looks from the other two operators. "Well, they did, but she's being moved. Their asset will make contact once they know exactly where she has been taken. He thinks it's likely north, away from Beirut, and possibly into Syria."

"So, what are the Israelis doing?" asked Dalton.

"Nothing. It's on us now."

The American looked at Kryton unsurely.

"They will share all intelligence with us, but they need to remove any attribution to their asset. It has to look like we found out through other means, so they won't get involved; either diplomatically or otherwise."

"Otherwise?" asked Dalton.

"As in non-diplomatic options," stated Cav. "If there is a recovery option available, it'll be up to us."

"Okay," said Dalton. "That's what we want, isn't it?"

"No, mate, it's exactly what we don't want. What we want is for her to be released, and then get the hell out of Lebanon," replied Kryton as he folded the paper up and slid it into his pocket.

"I'll call the driver up," said Dalton, before getting up and moving outside to make contact with the CIA officer located nearby.

Cav also went to get up, but noticed Kryton looking at the ground with a confused look on his face.

"What is it?"

Kryton looked up.

"Levy said something that reminded me of something else, but I can't quite recall what it was," he said.

"About?"

"About how I folded up the newspaper," replied Kryton.

"Umm...the what?"

Kryton just shook his head dismissively.

"Probably nothing," he said. "Let's just get back to the embassy and plan the next step."

16

Kryton and the team had a restless night waiting for the Israeli update. They knew that it wouldn't be quick, as the majority of Mossad tradecraft in the region was conducted old school – through direct human interaction and dead drops.

That took time. Patience would be the key.

The three stocky operators couldn't just sit around; it wasn't in their nature, so they killed some time through a very intense weights session. They each completed the sixty-minute workout in complete silence; solely focused on their own thoughts. Kryton still ran the operation over in his mind, trying to work out where it went wrong, and to work out how Jo could have been snatched so blatantly off of the street. His personal connection to her – both the intimate and the professional – made it particularly hard to think clearly. Perhaps he should have never let her be part of that particular operation?

Maybe; but she was a professional. Like the others, she was trained, and she knew the risks. Deep down, he knew she would never forgive him by treating her with kid gloves. He decided to attempt to destroy the heavy bag with ten minutes of solo boxing. He was almost finished when he saw someone attempting to grab his attention out of the corner of his eye. It was one of the CIA analysts.

"Sir, you have an urgent call in the SCIF," said the young female.

Kryton simply nodded his head to acknowledge her. He grabbed his towel and smashed down half a bottle of water, then proceeded to follow her out of the gym, down the covered walkway, and back into the small CIA annex. He entered the SCIF and was directed to the encrypted phone on one of the desks.

"Kryton," he said as he placed the handset next to his ear.

"It's Jonas, mate. We have a location provided by the Israelis."

Kryton's ears picked up at hearing this.

"Where?"

"The analyst should be bringing up the details on a map now. Langley received it and have forwarded it to us. They didn't waste any time," said Jonas.

"No, they didn't," replied Kryton, watching as the young, female analyst fiddled with the top-secret computer terminal to project a map onto the screen.

It was a large satellite map of the Middle East. The analyst zoomed in onto a location marked by a small red 'x'.

"That's in the south of Syria," said Kryton.

"Correct. The full memo has been forwarded to you; you can read it and get the details. It's in line with your meeting with Levy. It seems she has been taken by an element of Hezbollah. We're scrambling to raise every resource to try and determine their intent."

"Are we looking to negotiate this thing?" asked Kryton, concerned that it would be left to the diplomats, or worse, the politicians.

"We're unsure yet, mate. Our National Security Committee of Cabinet is meeting soon to discuss after they get briefed by the ASIS Director-General."

Kryton wiped some excess sweat off of his brow with his towel as he continued to look at the map.

"Will you be there for that meeting?"

"Yeah, mate," replied Jonas. "Tucked into the back wall somewhere; but I'll be in there."

"What are the yanks doing?"

"They're briefing their NSA about the same time. Fortunately, the president has a keen interest in us for obvious reasons, so he'll be updated at some point, I'm sure."

"What's happening right now?" Kryton then asked.

"CENTCOM will put some unmanned birds in the sky to start the recon. Keyhole satellites have been tasked to get current and historical footage to help build the int picture."

"And recovery options?" asked Kryton.

That was really the only question that Kryton cared about. He was essentially saying 'when are we going to stop stuffing around and go and get her?'

Jonas could tell that Kryton was frustrated.

"Options are being looked at. JSOC has a few available elements in the region that can be pulled off of task, mainly in the north of Syria. But it will take some time for them to get re-tasked, kitted properly, and complete a planning cycle."

"Fuck," mumbled Kryton under his breath as he turned around to find Cav and Dalton walk into the SCIF.

He was about to say something back to Jonas until he looked closely at Cav's sweat covered gym shirt. The words *Camp Baird Gymnasium* were wrapped around a logo of a muscle-bound kangaroo curling a dumbbell. Kryton allowed himself a small smile.

"We might have a closer option available. Let me make a quick call and I'll get back to you."

"Roger; call me in sixty-minutes. Things will start moving fast now," said Jonas.

Kryton ended the call and looked at his colleagues.

"We might have her location," he said without commitment.

Cav and Dalton looked at each other with more optimism than Kryton had.

"Where?" they both asked simultaneously.

He directed their attention to the screen, and to the small 'x' that marked the location that Israeli intelligence had told them that she was being held at.

"There."

"That's just up the road...sort of, anyway," exclaimed Dalton.

Kryton nodded in agreement.

"We going to go get her?" asked Cav, in a tone that suggested he couldn't believe they weren't already on the way there.

"The int agencies are trying to validate the Israeli info. Recon is being spun up to cover the location, and the yanks are probably going to take the lead in recovery," he said as he walked towards the SCIF door.

"Probably? What does that mean?" asked Cav.

"It means that I have to make a quick call first."

The two shooters looked at each other as Kryton departed the SCIF, grabbed his encrypted phone, and stepped into the open air to make a call. He placed the chunky looking phone next to his ear, and could hear the beeping digital noise as the phone attempted contact with the recipient. A few short dial tones later, an Australian voice answered.

"Rick Oates here."

"Mate, it's Kryton. Please tell me that you're still in the Middle East."

"Umm…yeah mate; we're in Jordan, about to head home."

Kryton allowed himself a small first pump.

"Don't get on the plane just yet. I might have something for you."

17

The fully armed and camouflaged soldiers sat in a neat, orderly row on fold out chairs facing the wall in a classified briefing room. The projector displayed various slides showing maps, intelligence information, as well as several pictures of Jo.

Kryton had just concluded the intelligence brief which would precede the combined SASR and Delta Force hostage recovery mission at a remote set of compounds in southern Syria. If the intelligence provided by the Israelis was accurate, Jo was being held there by an element of the Hezbollah terrorist organisation.

The combined task force had been formed at extremely short notice, drawing upon the tier one operators who were in the region undertaking other duties in various locations. The planning called for twenty-four shooters who would go onto the target, supported by enablers such as medics, signallers, a combat controller from the RAAF's 4 Squadron, as well as the Greyfin team.

Their task: rescue Jo.

The years of cross-training and cultural exchanges would enable the interoperability required to undertake the mission.

"Any questions?" asked Kryton as he completed the brief.

Rick Oates, Kryton's mate and the current intelligence officer assigned to the SASR team, raised his hand.

"Can you recap the expected enemy force size for us."

It was the only question most of the highly qualified and experienced operators really cared about. In essence, the question was really 'how many guys will we have to kill on target?'

"The UAV has been undertaking recon all day over the target, and it appears very quiet. Additional information from special partner reporting indicates that we're expecting between five to six tangoes."

The brief didn't require attribution of the source of the intelligence to the Israelis. One of the more analytically minded shooters then raised his hand.

"Has the hostage actually been confirmed on target?" he asked.

"No...not yet. This is viable foreign intelligence based off of what we assess is reliable HUMINT reporting."

A dull murmur filled the room as the operators started talking amongst themselves. Kryton looked at Oates, who just shrugged his shoulders. The two intelligence soldiers were used to this response when briefing special forces operators, who despite nearly twenty years of combat, still for some reason couldn't comprehend that intelligence rarely provide a full picture. It was understandable, though. Although they hungered for action, the highly skilled soldiers wanted to ensure that they only risked their lives for a purposeful outcome. With no other questions forthcoming, the briefing was concluded.

"Wheels up in thirty minutes," the young SASR captain instructed.

The audience stood up to commence their final preparations. They all knew their roles. Four U.S. Army Blackhawks would travel the nearly 200 kilometres in darkness to the target south-east of Damascus. The Jordanian government had given approval for the operation to be launched from their air base, on the tacit approval that their logistical involvement be kept secret.

Nearly thirty thousand feet above the target, a USAF Predator drone circled the location of the compounds where the Israelis had said Jo was, being guided by a pilot sitting comfortably in a non-descript shipping container at a USAF base in Germany. Kryton nodded at Dalton as the two men helped themselves to a sandwich from the table in the corner. Other operators either had some coffee, or just drank some water. Each man had his own pre-mission routine. One Delta operator was even doing push-ups outside of the briefing room.

"Okay, let's go get her," said Kryton as he picked up his helmet and walked to the flight line.

Cav and Dalton stuck to his tail. Their eyes narrowed as they focused on the mission ahead. A loadmaster was waiting for them on the tarmac, and the various operators peeled off into their respective chalk groups and waited his instructions. Kryton let the warm night air wash across his face. The familiar whine of the turbine engines was soon followed by the well-known whacking sounds of the rotor blades commencing their circular movements. The loadmaster waited for the call from the pilot to come across the radio headset. His expensive helmet was full of modern technology, including cutting edge night vision. It reminded Kryton of something out of a science fiction movie.

A minute later, the loadmaster raised his hand and directed the assault team to move towards their respective birds. The various operators loaded onto the choppers and secured themselves to the deck. Kryton could hear over the radio net as all of the teams called in stating that they were ready. Less than two minutes later, the birds were airborne and moving in a diamond formation towards Syria.

Displayed on various television screens in secure buildings at several different places across the world, the live footage from the Predator drone indicated a general level of inactivity around the target. Analysts at both the JSOC annex at CENTCOM HQ in Tampa, Florida, as well as at Greyfin HQ in Canberra, studied the various intelligence feeds that contributed to the mission.

Nearly forty minutes later, the airborne convoy crossed the Syrian border, descending to the desert floor and extinguishing their navigation lights. Despite years of civil war, the Syrian military still possessed a formidable anti-air capability, so they would have to ensure that they stayed well below the Syrian air-detection systems.

JSOC controlled the mission from their secure compound inside CENTCOM HQ, and provided fused data that advised the team of updated intelligence, such as new threats and current activity at the target site. The assault leader intermittently updated the team as they progressed.

"Thirty minutes out…"

"Twenty minutes out…"

"Ten minutes out…"

The pilots made gradual turns to avoid the many hills and wadis that littered the desert floor. The stars provided just enough light for Kryton to make out the various features through his NVGs.

"Two minutes out," soon came the call over the radio.

On each of the choppers, the operators held two fingers up to acknowledge the call. They unfastened the clips that secured them to the deck, and slowly moved to position to disembark rapidly upon landing. Kryton wriggled his fingers to stretch them out, before taking a more secure grip of his M-4 carbine rifle. He slightly adjusted the NVGs over his helmet and twisted his head from side to side to stretch his neck. It was just a habit that served little purpose apart from helping to synchronise his body and his mind to the task ahead, similar to a tennis player bouncing the ball several times before serving.

"Thirty seconds," came the call.

The loadmaster peered over his M-60 machine gun as the helicopter made its final descent. He held his hand up towards the passengers as he watched the wheels slowly touch the flat, rocky surface. He quickly dropped his arm in a chopping motion, indicating that that it was time to go. In a well drilled and rapid movement, the assault team exited the aircraft and moved towards its front, quickly spreading out and taking a knee. They now formed an arc providing protection for the helicopter, as well as each other

Three helicopters had touched down, whilst the fourth – fitted with specialist equipment and medics in case of the requirement of a medivac – stayed airborne mere feet above the ground. Within a minute, all of the birds were airborne again, and moved off in formation to the south and away from the assault team. Kryton looked around through his NVGs, seeing all of the other operators on their knees and with their weapons raised, looking for potential threats. An additional few minutes later, the whirring of the rotor blades was replaced by the eerie silence of the remoteness of the Syrian desert. The team stayed in position for roughly ten minutes, waiting to see if their arrival had attracted any local attention. After the planned wait time, Kryton stood and moved over to the assault commander. He kneeled next to the young army captain and whispered in his ear.

"No new updates."

The young officer nodded, before looking around to get the attention of his counterpart in the Delta Force component, who acknowledged with a thumbs up.

"Okay, move now," he said quietly into the radio.

They were not on target just yet.

The team had deliberately chosen a remote and unpopulated spot five kilometres from the compound. They would walk up onto the target. A highly visible and noisy assault risked having the hostage killed before they could be rescued, so a more discreet insertion method was chosen instead. The team stood and started walking in a pre-planned formation, taking just over an hour to walk to the form-up point close to the target. Despite the relative coolness of the evening, they were all sweating profusely by the time they arrived.

Several dull lights emanated from the four, single-story buildings, suggesting that there were occupants present. Kryton lied down next to the young captain and looked at his watch. It was just before midnight. The operation was still adhering to the planned timings. The compound only had a knee-high fence around it, and covered about one-hundred square metres. There were a few smaller sheds scattered amongst some fig trees. The GEOINT analysts had prepared some amazingly in-depth pictures to enable the planning, and had even been able to determine the depth of the creeks and the gradient of the ground surrounding the location. The operators moved quietly into position, in most cases crawling across the ground that was a mixture of sand, rock, and dry scrub. Kryton observed the main building where they assessed Jo would most likely be.

Three figures suddenly appeared from behind its corner. Each appeared to be carrying an assault rifle, which through the NVGs looked to be AK variants. Their voices carried across the night air, and Kryton could tell that they were speaking Arabic. Within a moment, they returned inside. Due to the size of the target area, the plan called for an approach from two sides in order to reduce the likelihood of fratricide. Kryton, Cav, and Dalton would provide cover to the SASR and Delta assault teams, who had polished their methodologies and tactics through years of practice as a team at both Campbell Barracks and Fort Bragg respectively.

"Bravo team ready," came the quiet voice over the radio.

The captain looked at Kryton and nodded.

"Go," the young officer said quietly.

Twenty-four figures emerged from the shadows and moved quickly and purposefully towards the compound; their weapons were raised and infra-red beams of light pointed at the target, visible only through their night vision.

Cav viewed a lone figure walking between the buildings through the scope of his sniper rifle as the team approached the target. He adjusted for the man's direction and gait, allowing just enough of a lead for his supressed rifle to drop the unsuspecting target on the first shot.

A dog started barking, attracted to the man's lifeless body slumping to the ground and disturbing the quiet of the night. The assault team quickened their approach, and were now less than forty metres from the target. The darkness covered their movements, which would have been all but impossible in daylight due to the minimal natural concealment.

Suddenly, a loud shout cried out. This sound was nothing compared to the ear shattering noise of a fully automatic machine gun opening up which quickly followed. The belt-fed weapon strewed searing hot metal across the path of the American and Australian soldiers.

"What the fuck?" said Kryton, his querying comment interrupted by the sound of a second machine gun also opening up.

"PKMs; two of them, to the north side concealed in the sheds," said Cav across the radio, having quickly identified the locations of the Soviet era weapons from their muzzle flashes.

The SASR team hit the deck and started digging in with their eye lashes. The 7.62-millimetre rounds struck the dirt mere metres from the Australians. However, the firing appeared to be indiscriminate, and likely in panicked reaction to the killing of the lone guard.

The Greyfin men watched as several tangoes rapidly exited the main compound, raising their AKs at the darkness and firing blindly. The three operators took aim, each dropping a terrorist in quick succession with a well-aimed shot. The PKMs continued firing, halting the advance of the Australian element.

"We can't progress," came the desperate voice of the young captain through the radio over the sound of the gunfire his own troops were sending back down range.

"Bravo is clearing second building, but we're also getting resistance," said the Delta commander, indicating that the Americans were also dealing with their own issues.

"What the fuck?" said Kryton again.

He rolled to his side and switched the radio net to call back to the SOCCE.

"Eagle Alpha; this is Dingo One. We're getting significant resistance. How's your view from above?"

The military and intelligence personnel in Tampa looked dumbfounded as they watched multiple heat signatures come pouring out of the buildings and sheds of the compound like angry wasps from their disturbed nest.

"Multiple enemy personnel now on target location. The majority are to your north and west," they informed Kryton.

"Roger. Can you give us a number?"

The analysts continued to look at the screen to try to give an estimate.

"Dingo One, we're tracking up to twenty-five tangoes."

"Holy fuck," he muttered.

Dalton looked at him, seeking an update.

"The intelligence is shit. We've got about two-dozen enemy," said Kryton, as Cav dropped yet another tango with his long rifle.

Kryton passed the updated detail to the rest of the assault team.

"I wish we could nuke those gun pits from above," mulled Dalton, with the coolness of a seasoned operator who was going through this not for the first time.

In Iraq and Afghanistan, the many 'Kill or Capture' missions undertaken by the various coalition special forces units were often supported by UAVs armed with missiles. If the attack became too hot, they would look to flatten the target with high-explosive ordnance. That wasn't viable in a hostage rescue, though.

"Alright," said Kryton, contemplating the situation. "We're going to have to flank them from the west and ease the pressure on the sas-cats. Dalton, you're with me. Cav, you stay here and provide cover."

18

The two Greyfin operators informed the SASR captain of their intentions, then moved towards the western edge of the compound. The PKMs continued their relentless rate of fire, suggesting that the terrorists had a decent supply of ammunition.

Kryton and Dalton moved in a tight formation, with their weapons raised and infra-red lasers pointed at the wall of the building they were fast approaching. They reached the corner of it, and could now see where the muzzle flash of the first PKM was coming out through a window opening.

"Frag?" asked Dalton.

Kryton nodded, stepping slightly away from the building wall to cover the SEAL. Dalton pulled the pin on the grenade and – in between muzzle flashes – lobbed it through the window, after which the two men immediately turned their back away from the window by hugging the wall. A dull thud was followed by a bright flash as the grenade's explosives violently spewed out hundreds of razor-sharp metal fragments.

They immediately stood up and moved back towards the door of the building. Dalton kicked it in, stepping to the side just enough to allow Kryton to make first entry. They enacted their well-rehearsed two-man CQB drills, quickly firing two rounds into the seemingly lifeless bodies sitting at the base of the now mangled machined gun.

"First gun down," said Kryton across the net.

He then heard a click behind him, before quickly swinging around to find in the blackened corner of the small building a similarly sized man desperately trying to clear a stoppage on his AK rifle. Kryton's heart skipped a beat as he quickly processed that the man had somehow avoided their sweep of the room – which was reasonable considering the mess that the grenade had caused – and had been able to aim his rifle at the Australian, only failing to kill the intruder because of poor weapon maintenance.

Dalton finished the man off with two quick rounds to the chest.

Kryton looked at him. Even through the NVGs, the American sailor could see Kryton's mouth agape from what could have been.

"I got your back, Aussie," he said calmly, in a brief moment of levity.

They looked out of the same window where the PKM had been firing through, and could see the muzzle flash of the second belt-fed machine gun still raking the ground where the SASR soldiers were approaching from. The reduction in lethal enemy fire by fifty percent had allowed a small number of Australians to leopard crawl their way to the building with the remaining PKM. After getting under its barrel, they proceeded to conduct the same assault drill that Kryton and Dalton had just successfully utilised.

With the use of two grenades, they silenced the PKM, and then the four-man team cleared the building of the remaining terrorists. The remaining SASR team then continued with their assault, storming the main building and conducting room clearance drills on the mud-brick structure. Almost every room had a terrorist inside it, some having been caught in a daze from all of the confusion. Sporadic gunfire could be heard as the Delta team continued their own assault. Radio calls peppered the net as the teams cleared their assigned buildings. Kryton lost count of how many dead tangoes were being called through.

But so far, no word of the hostage.

With the PKMs now neutralised, Cav moved from his cover and took a kneeling position closer to the target, still picking off the terrorists who aimlessly exited the safety of their buildings and into the deadly open ground of the night air. Without having adjusted night vision to help guide them, they were easy targets.

Jonas watched on his screen at Greyfin HQ as the battle evolved, seeing the flashing infra-red strobe lights of friendly troops mingled amongst the heat signatures of the terrorists.

"Jesus Christ," he mumbled, placing his hands on his hips in disbelief.

Disbelief very quickly turned to anger. He turned to one of his U.S. analysts.

"Get me the CIA LO at JSOC," he demanded.

Back in Syria, the combined special operations team were slowly taking back the initiative, methodically clearing the buildings and rooms, whilst suffering very few casualties. That itself was remarkable considering what they had stumbled on. Within fifteen minutes, all gunfire had ceased. Kryton ran into the main building, linking up with the senior enlisted soldier from the SASR team.

"What the fuck, Zach? This was like Tizak. Where did this intel come from?"

The veteran SASR sergeant was right to be pissed by comparing the assault to the Battle of Tizak in Afghanistan in 2010 – a battle where intelligence had indicated that a small number of insurgents would be conducting a shura with their commander, which in fact turned out to be a major Taliban conference involving over one-hundred well-armed and skilled insurgent fighters. Kryton was also pissed, but he had other priorities at the moment.

"Where is she?" he desperately asked the sergeant.

"Still clearing the target. No sign yet."

That didn't make sense. It was a relatively small target, so they should have found her by now. Kryton was terrified that the loss of surprise might have given the terrorists enough time to extract her to another location...or worse. Once they were confident that they owned the battlefield, Kryton called Cav over.

"Ask the choppers if they had any squirters," he said, before proceeding off with the SASR sergeant to have closer look for Jo.

Cav nodded, then spoke into his radio to have a short conversation with the lead pilot of the Blackhawks. Their role had been to stay off to the north and intercept any escaping terrorists – or squirters – who might have attempted to escape. That hadn't been anticipated as likely based on the size the of the opposing force in the Israeli intelligence, but after what they had just experienced, anything could have happened.

Cav also checked with the UAV team, who replied that they hadn't observed anyone getting away. Everyone who was on the target during the assault was still there – either dead or alive.

Kryton stood by the building and called the respective team leaders over whilst the operators conducted the SSE. Any intelligence they discovered might not relate to their specific mission, but could assist the agencies to better understand other regional terrorist groups.

"One final check?" he pleaded with the SASR team leader.

The young captain, trying to balance the operational risk with the operational objective, agreed. They were still inside an adversarial country, so they needed to get airborne as quick as possible.

"Okay. But if we can't find her within the next few minutes, we have to get the hell out of dodge."

Kryton gave the thumbs up and ran off with Cav to search some of the smaller buildings. Other members of Delta were doing the same, even ripping up carpets to look for trapdoors and pulling items off of the walls to look for concealed hides – all lessons that had been learned fighting the cunning jihadis in Iraq. Ten minutes later, having searched every possible location, and with reports from the UAV of vehicles headed in their direction, the team leader called the birds back in.

"We have to go," the army officer said firmly.

Kryton nodded. Dalton soon joined the two Australian Greyfin soldiers, feeling just as disheartened as both of them.

"There's nothing to suggest someone has been kept here as a hostage. No blood; no clothing of hers; not even some strands of hair. The Delta boys were pretty thorough; they do this sort of thing all the time, and they know what to look for," Dalton said over the increasing noise of the approaching Blackhawks.

Kryton couldn't form any words. He had never in all his life felt as helpless as he did at that moment. The only lead they had had proven to be nothing, and had resulted in some minor injuries to a few soldiers. The entire assault team loaded back onto the Blackhawks and commenced their return to the Jordanian air base. Medics worked on the wounded soldiers, but fortunately there were no serious injuries. Kryton slumped in his seat, devastated. Thirty minutes later, the formation of choppers crossed the border and back into Jordanian airspace. He remained lost in his thoughts until one of the loadmasters tapped him on the leg, lowering his helmet mic to shout over the noise.

"There's a call for you over the external net," said the American airman, handing Kryton the cable to insert into his own headset.

Kryton listened to the voice on the other end. His instant perkiness attracted the attention of Cav and Dalton.

"Map," he said to Dalton, holding his hand out.

The SEAL drew the planning map from his leg pocket and handed it to Kryton, who intently made some calculations in his head. The Australian then shuffled over next to the loadmaster and had a quick conversation, also talking to the pilot and the SASR team leader. The whole interaction only took a few minutes, concluding when each of them gave a thumbs up of acknowledgement. Kryton leaned back into his seat and let out a deep sigh of relief as the SASR troopers received a quick briefing from their boss. The helicopter quickly banked to the west in a change of course.

"What the fuck?" said Cav, as both he and Dalton demanded their own brief.

Kryton leaned in to form a tight circle with his mates.

"We've got her. She's safe and well. We're going to pick her up. No hostile parties on site," he briefed them, in a complete change of demeanour.

Cav and Dalton looked at each other, both excited but confused.

"You're not going to believe what happened," Kryton added, noticing their confusion. "But let's get our girl and make sure she's safe."

A little over an hour later, the lone helicopter, guided by the UAV still supporting the new mission, landed at a remote area near the Syrian and Israeli border. Having being fully briefed on the task, the SASR troopers exited the helicopter and formed a quick perimeter around the aircraft. A set of headlights from a tattered four-wheeled drive Jeep illuminated two figures – one who was clearly a woman.

Kryton quickly jumped off of the aircraft and legged it at full speed to the two silhouettes. Cav and Dalton struggled to keep up with him. As he got closer, he could clearly see that one of the people was Jo. Kryton shouldered his weapon and gently grabbed her by the arms, looking at her up and down like a parent who had just found a lost child. His relief was palpable. He tried to speak, but a slurry of words just came out. He quickly composed himself and spoke again.

"I'm so sorry, Jo."

Despite looking a little ragged and tired, she appeared none the worse for wear. She returned a curious gaze, clearly wondering why he would say that. She certainly didn't blame him for what had happened, and she felt nothing but gratefulness for the fact they had come to get her. She smiled at him, placing her right hand on his chest in an attempt to reassure him.

"I'm okay...really," she said.

Cav and Dalton quickly joined them, with both men also patting her on the back and welcoming her return. They, too, were relieved to see her back in one piece. Cav looked at the man standing off to the side who was with Jo when they landed. He looked at him for a moment curiously, trying to place the somewhat familiar face.

Then he remembered.

"Shit. Isn't that the guy from...?"

"Yes, it is," said Jo, cutting him off. "I'll explain later. We need to get out of here before the sun comes up, and he needs to get back before they know he's missing."

Cav was even more confused now, but before he could speak Kryton started guiding them back to the chopper.

"We'll back brief in Jordan," he said.

The team returned to the helicopter and quickly boarded. A medic started looking over Jo. Apart from some bruises and scratches, she appeared to be in good health, and at worst a little dehydrated. The noise of the engine increased in pitch as the pilot returned his steed to the night sky. The first traces of nautical twilight could be seen over the eastern horizon as they once again headed south and back to the air base. Jo looked out of the open door of the Blackhawk and waved at the man as he returned to the Jeep. The colour started returning to Kryton's face, which had been pale white for the past few days. He allowed himself a few moments to enjoy the relief of Jo's return, and then turned his attention once again to the original mission.

Cav leaned in and shouted over the whirling rotors.

"What's next?"

Kryton took a sip from his water bottle, which quickly turned to several gulps as he realised just how dehydrated he had been from the assault on the target.

"We make sure Jo's okay. Then we're back on task."

Cav and Dalton both gave the thumbs up.

"But, first," added Kryton stoically, "we need to pay a visit to our Israeli friends."

19

The children played in the hot sand as their parents laid back on the deck chairs which were lined up in rows along the water's edge. The afternoon sun drew crowds of locals and tourists alike to cool off in the water or tan their bodies using copious amounts of coconut oil.

Amongst it all, a lone figure sat on the footpath overlooking the playfulness, enjoying the westerly breeze as it washed over his face. He looked down at his watch.

1630.

He took one last, deep puff of his cigarette and took one final glance of the happy scene in front of him, before moving off and up the road to his planned rendezvous. He reached a narrow side street and walked down it, walking past the bins and random cats that lined the back of the apartment buildings. He soon reached a doorway nestled between two large stacks of milk crates, entering it and closing the door behind him.

The otherwise empty, dusty room was illuminated only by a slither of light provided by an elongated window near the roof, with a table and several chairs in the middle. The man observed a person sitting at the table with their back turned to him. He frowned as he walked to the middle of the room, and started speaking in Hebrew.

"What happened? You were supposed to get her back to Beirut safely. Where the hell is she?"

Jacob Levy sat down at the table to face the person who he had a planned meeting with. His face dropped when he saw that it was, in fact, not the person now sitting opposite him. He was about to get up when the clicking, metallic sound of pistol being cocked from the shadows behind him made him stop.

"Perhaps you should stay seated," said Kryton as he pulled the rope string to turn on the single light bulb sitting above the table. "You seem

110

surprised to see me; were you expecting someone else?" he added playfully.

Levy sat down. The Mossad officer adjusted his position in his seat and inhaled deeply, trying to re-establish the balance of power.

Kryton was having none of it.

"You're on home turf having a pre-arranged meeting with an asset with minimal exposure or risk; you have no support outside; there is no-one coming to help you."

Levy tried to keep a stoic face, but the slightest twitch of his eyebrow betrayed the fact that he knew that he had clearly been outplayed. He looked at Kryton frustratedly, then slumped his shoulders in acceptance of his predicament.

"Did you kill my asset?" he asked the Australian.

Kryton shook his head in the negative.

"Are you here to kill me?" he then asked.

Kryton allowed the question to hang in the air for a moment. Even for a seasoned professional like Levy, the silence was deafening, and forced him to consider, if only for a second, that this stingy little room in an old warehouse might be the last place he ever saw.

"No," finally replied Kryton. "Unlike your masters, we don't do assassination."

Levy breathed a deep sigh of relief. He knew that if they were going to kill him, he'd probably be dead already. It certainly wasn't the first time in his career he had had to ask the question, though.

"But that was not *my* decision, of course," added Kryton.

The added venom in this statement displayed Kryton's current feelings towards the Israeli spy. Jo had been unfortunate enough to be in a part of the world where the Mossad were conducting their own operation. Whilst following Popov, she had recognised one of the assassins. Levy had wasted no time getting his officers back into the field after he collected them from the CIA safehouse in Dubai, and seeing again the female spy she had fought in the loading dock of the shopping mall had simply been a case of wrong place at the wrong time, so they decided to kidnap her to avoid a potential compromise of their own mission.

The Israeli's had treated her well, knowing that they would have to let her go at some point. They used her as a ruse to get a so-called ally to risk their own people to eliminate a terrorist cell by getting the Australians to believe that she had been captured by Hezbollah. The

111

intelligence chiefs of both the U.S. and Australia had intensely pondered over the past forty-eight hours why Israel would deliberately risk such a valuable alliance; but the reasons why would have to come later, and would be dealt with at a much higher level than the two people right now sitting under a flimsy light bulb in Tel Aviv.

"Is your girl okay?" asked Levy, trying to build some rapport with the Australian.

Kryton tilted his head as he looked at the Israeli apathetically.

"Why don't you ask her?" he said, looking over Levy's shoulder.

The Mossad officer turned his head and watched as Jo moved out of the shadows of the corner of the room and into the light, pointing an Israeli made Jericho 941 at his head. The choice of weapon was by design – a statement to say that they were in charge, and to make Levy again question the fate of the asset he was supposed to be meeting. Jo didn't lower the pistol, and for a moment Levy wondered if her sentiments about assassination were indeed the same as Kryton's.

A small cough from Kryton ensured that she maintained her professionalism, and she lowered the weapon and sat down next to him, looking judgementally at Levy. Typically, it would feel awkward and tactically unwise to have their backs to the door, but the presence of Cav and Dalton outside would ensure that they would remain undisturbed.

The two Australians looked at the Israeli for a moment in silence, letting him sweat it out, before Kryton decided it was time to get down to business.

"You said in Dubai that you were not our adversary. What you say next will determine whether I believe that."

Levy sat upright, before nodding in agreement.

"Why did you lie about knowing her location and send us to Syria?"

Levy was firm in his reply, and certainly unapologetic.

"An opportunity presented itself to remove a violent and dangerous terrorist cell that was responsible for several attacks on Israeli citizens."

Kryton pulled a piece of paper from his jacket pocket. He read it aloud.

"Ah, yes; the Glorious Martyrs Brigade. An offshoot of Hezbollah. Why didn't you just take care of them yourselves?"

Levy interlocked his fingers as he sat forward in his seat.

"It would have compromised a significant asset we have inside Hezbollah. One who we intend on continuing to use. We won't justify to anyone protecting our national interests. We treated you well, didn't we?" said Levy, looking at Jo.

Jo glared at Levy.

"I suppose," she replied.

Levy sat back with a renewed smugness on his face.

"So, you thought using an American special operations team to do it instead would be the answer!?"

The smug look quickly disappeared. Levy glanced at Jo, then back at Kryton. He appeared genuinely confused.

"Oh, that's right, you don't know. Well, Mister Levy, you might have a working relationship with the Americans, but *we* have the friendship. You were mistaken if you thought that they would simply pass on the intel you provided them to us. We're here because we're working *with* them. There happened to be a JSOC team with us on our little jaunt inside Syria, and they are not too happy with you right now," said Kryton.

Levy had to think for a moment. Rubbing Australia the wrong way was one thing, but to screw over their largest and most important ally would have deeper consequences.

"That will be an issue for my government to sort out with the Americans at a higher level," he replied dismissively.

"And with my government, too?" asked Kryton.

Levy didn't have a ready answer for that question. But Kryton did.

"Well, let me tell you what both the U.S. and Australian ambassadors are telling your Foreign Minister sometime today. The billion-dollar military communications contracts that were about to be signed for the U.S. and Australian Defence Departments are going to be torn up. They won't publicly go into a great detail as to why, but suffice it to say, I imagine that your boss at Mossad will be getting a phone call not long after seeking some answers. You were warned after forging Australian passports to conduct your wet work in Dubai to leave us out of your operations."

Kryton let that sit with Levy for a moment. The Israeli sat back and pursed his lips. It was a diplomatic consequence, but one that would have internal ramifications. Whilst the decision to kidnap Jo and conduct the ruse had likely been approved at the highest levels within the Mossad, they still had to answer to their political masters who couldn't afford to put the Americans offside. He looked at Jo. The veteran spy still had a small ethical streak.

"For what it's worth, I am sorry. It was an operational call."

She looked at him, sensing some sincerity in his voice. She glanced at Kryton and gave him a small nod, as if to say that she accepted it was time to move on. He took her cue, and once again reached into his jacket pocket, pulling out a postcard sized photo. He placed it face up on the table and slid it across to Levy.

It was a CCTV picture of Boyd. Despite the recent interruptions, the Greyfin team had returned to their original mission. Levy looked at the picture, then back up at the two Australians sitting in front of him. For a microsecond, he thought about playing coy, but his experience told him that if this was a game of chess, he was nowhere near winning. He also felt a sense of relief, knowing that the Australians still needed information that he possessed.

He would not be dying today.

He pushed the photo back towards Kryton. Realising that he was on the backfoot and needing to quickly repair the now damaged relationship, he decided to give them whatever they were after.

"What do you want to know?"

"We know he's one of yours. He might not have come up on any of our systems like your other agents did, but he's definitely with you. He murdered someone in Australia, and we've spent quite a bit of time trying to find him. Who is he? Why did you assassinate someone on our land?" asked Kryton.

Levy leaned forward and started to speak.

"A few months back, an asset of ours inside Russian intelligence made contact to inform us that he had some highly sensitive information regarding a sleeper cell of agents that Russia had placed across western nations. These men are scientists by trade, but they are trained by the FSB."

Kryton looked at Jo, who returned his intrigued look. Since Beirut, Kryton had suspected that the Israelis knew about the Russian scientists. This now proved it.

"Why did he tell *you* this? Why didn't he go to the Americans?" asked Kryton.

"This asset is a Russian Jew. His motivations are, how would you say…ideological. He shared that information in exchange for asylum for his brother who was fighting in Ukraine."

"And?" probed Kryton.

"And, we gave the man asylum. The brother – our asset – is a military intelligence officer who worked for the FSB before getting called back into military service for the Ukraine operation. He had previously worked on the illegals project."

Despite the Cold War having long finished, it was widely known in the western intelligence community that the Russians still ran long term sleeper agents inside the U.S. and other Anglophone nations.

"What was their purpose?" asked Jo.

"Initially, it was to infiltrate various nuclear related programs, in the U.S., Australia, and Europe, and to learn about advancements in technology, and to disrupt, if required, any new programs."

"Initially?" asked Kryton.

"Yes, well," replied Levy, turning his head to see a shelf with several water bottles on it, "umm, may I have some water first?" he segued.

Kryton nodded, and Jo stood to retrieve three bottles, placing them down on the table. Levy opened a bottle and took a long sip. Kryton wondered for a moment if he might be stalling, but he was too curious to see what the Israeli had to say to interrupt what might simply be his patter. Levy quickly continued his brief.

"Initially, that was their purpose. However, on interrogation of one of that sleeper cell who we captured in… well, let's just say we captured him… led us to intelligence that they were in fact looking to support rogue nations develop nuclear capabilities. Their CIA handlers would be asking for their knowledge on Russian nuclear activities, not investigating them personally."

"Rogue nations?" asked Jo.

"Yes. North Korea; Venezuela; and…"

"And Iran," said Kryton, completing the thought, and now understanding why the Israelis hadn't told the Americans.

Iran had long been considered in Israeli political, military, and intelligence circles as being the Jewish state's greatest threat. Their policy was to deal with this threat any way that was required.

And in most cases, unilaterally.

Kryton rubbed his hand over his face and thought for a moment. It did appear that the Israelis were not the adversary here. It also confirmed that the intelligence systems that had been assumed to be hacked to compromise the identity of the scientists hadn't been hacked after all.

That would ease some minds in Washington and Canberra.

Kryton needed some direction before proceeding. He whispered into his radio for Dalton to come inside and replace him. The frogman soon entered the room, and sat down next to Jo whilst Kryton went outside and met up with Cav.

"I need to talk to Jonas" he said, motioning for the commando to hand him the satellite phone.

Kryton initiated a call and waited as the connection was relayed across the globe through several satellites.

"So, what did he say?" asked Cav, seeking an update.

Kryton exhaled deeply as his eyes continued to adjust to the outside light.

"Well, it certainly seems like they knew about the Russians through other means. It's part of some other op they had going. It's all coincidence, but certainly related. It seems that the Russians are sleep agents after all."

"You suspected that they were involved in some way. How?"

Kryton smiled.

"Remember when we met Levy in Beirut? He admonished me for accidently using an abort signal using a newspaper. That same signal was used by Boyd in Dubai when you and Jo were about to grab him. I didn't think much more about it at the time because we were focused on getting Jo back."

Cav chuckled as he learned of the connection.

Spies and their bullshit games, he thought to himself.

"Jonas? Yeah, it's me," said Kryton as the phone finally connected to Greyfin HQ on the other side of the world. "Our suspicions are correct. They're involved, but not directly. It *is* a sleeper cell. The Israelis have one of the scientists captured; that's how they found out. If Levy isn't bullshitting us again, and I think he might not be this time, then the Russians were sent to help some nasty third world countries develop their nuke capability. What do we do now?"

Kryton listened to the directions from Jonas for several minutes, before clarifying and acknowledging the plan. He terminated the call and looked at Cav.

"Well, hang on to your hat. We're going to be working with them now."

Cav's jaw dropped.

"Are you kidding me? I'm surprised we haven't heard shots from inside there from Dalton putting two rounds into that prick's face. He was as pissed about what happened to Jo as you were."

Kryton placed a hand on his mate's broad shoulder.

"This is the game we play, mate. Besides, there's bigger issues to focus on right now."

Cav looked at Kryton in a dismayed manner, but knew that there was no point protesting. They both worked for people much higher up the food chain than they were, and explanations were not always forthcoming. Kryton returned to the room and swapped out with Dalton. He sat down and looked at Levy.

"My superiors are interested to know more about what you know. It would seem our interests are now aligned. Far from adversarial…wouldn't you agree?"

Levy sat for a moment, glancing at Jo, and then back at Kryton.

"I would. What do you propose?"

Kryton leaned into the table.

"I've been directed to work with you to resolve this issue. However, there are three things I want before we go there: Firstly, what is the name of the Russian scientist you captured and interrogated? We need to validate your level of knowledge."

Levy smiled. It was a fair question, and he knew it might go some way to regaining Mossad's credibility.

"His name was Igor Sokolov. He told us all the details about the sleeper cell and their work. From there, we initiated our operation to remove them and the threat that they posed."

"His name *was?*" asked Jo, curious as to why the Israeli had utilised past tense.

The look Levy gave back suggested that she didn't want to know.

"Secondly, do you know where the fifth and last scientist is?" asked Kryton.

Levy slowly reached into his pocket and drew a pack of cigarettes out. He looked at Kryton for approval, and upon getting it, lit one and drew deeply on it.

"No, we don't I'm afraid," he said.

The tone of his voice – one of reluctant admission – suggested to Kryton that he was being truthful.

"And I suspect that you don't, either," said Levy, offering the pack of cigarettes to Kryton and Jo, both of whom politely declined.

The two Australians glanced at each other. Their body language was enough for Levy to have his suspicions confirmed.

"So, the scientists in Australia; in Germany; in Lebanon. That was all your people?" asked Kryton, looking to get back to the task rather than dwell on their respective intelligence shortcomings

Levy nodded. Now it all clicked into place. It was certainly ballsy and without regard for the sovereignty of other nations. But, as Kryton had considered earlier, Israel often acted brashly in its own self-interests – a necessary requirement of being the world's only Jewish state, located in the middle of millions of angry displaced people, all caused by the lack of foresight or understanding by western powers nearly a century earlier.

"And the third thing?" asked Levy, taking another drag of the pungent, Arabic made cigarette.

Kryton placed his hand on the CCTV image of Boyd – or at least the person they only knew as Boyd – and pushed it back in front of Levy.

"Who is he?"

Levy didn't need to look at the photo again. He extinguished the cigarette onto the corner of the table and looked back at Kryton.

"Would you like to meet him?"

******

Twenty minutes later, the Greyfin team exited the barren building, having come to an agreement with Levy. They hastily made their way east and towards the more urban area away from the beach.

A white Mercedes-Benz van came screeching up beside them as they turned the corner of a quiet street, almost knocking Cav and Dalton over.

"Bloody hell," exclaimed Cav as he leaned on Dalton to right himself after tripping on the curb.

A large, bearded face appeared from the front passenger's side window.

"Sorry about that team; we got caught in the traffic," said Kryton's mentor, Adam Johns.

The rear sliding door was opened, and the team quickly hustled to get inside before the driver quickly sped off.

"Sorted?" Johns asked.

"Sorted," replied Kryton, fastening his seatbelt from the middle seats.

Johns nodded his head and turned his attention to Jo.

118

"How are you?" he asked in a paternally affectionate manner.

Jo returned his large smile.

"Good…thanks to you," she replied.

"Meh…it's just fortunate that I know certain people," he said self-depreciatively, before looking at the driver of their van. "Isn't that right, mate?"

The driver looked back at Johns and smiled.

"Of course, boss," he said.

The driver was, by now, familiar to all of them. A man who they had first seen – without suspicion – during the initial meeting with Levy when he had driven the Israeli spy to RV with Greyfin at the CIA safehouse near Dubai. An Arab man who, although an Israeli asset, was in fact once the interpreter – as well as being an agent – for Johns' special forces team during the early days of the Iraq war. When Levy had tasked him to guard Jo in a remote house near the Israeli and Syrian border until the coalition raid was completed on the terrorist cell, he had decided that his loyalty to his previous handler outweighed that to his current paymasters.

Of course, by now Levy was aware of who betrayed his operation and released Jo prematurely, but that didn't concern the Arab man as much as the safety of the young, female Australian did.

"I'm sure we can find some work for you instead," Johns said reassuringly.

The van moved through the bustling streets of Tel Aviv and towards the airport. They would look to return to Dubai in order to recalibrate, and plan the next moves.

"So, what *is* next?" asked Johns.

Kryton looked out of the window, taking a sip of water as he watched the people go about their afternoon business. He actually did appreciate the reasons why the Israelis conducted their business the way they did. He still couldn't help but shudder at the thought of how close they may have come to losing Jo.

"There's a rogue Russian scientist on the loose. We've been directed to find and capture him," said Kryton.

"How do we go about that?" asked Cav.

Kryton sighed as he looked back at his team.

"We've been chasing Boyd all this time. Now he's going to come to us."

20

Undisclosed location
Somewhere near Dubai
Thirty-Six hours later

Kryton once again found himself in the dawn hours waiting by an unused building in a remote part of the Dubai desert. The past two weeks were potentially about to culminate through a face-to-face meeting with the target of Greyfin's inaugural mission. An Israeli spy – nay, assassin – who had led them on a chase through the Middle East and into Europe.

The intelligence game is a fickle one, and it now appeared that a person once thought of as an enemy may now about to become an ally. That was the direction from above, at least. Kryton's experiences told him to err on the side of caution, and his most recent experiences – which almost got his team killed – once again left a bitter taste in his mouth. He would remain the consummate professional, however, and focus on the new mission at hand.

The Israeli intelligence regarding the nuclear scientists appeared legitimate on the surface, however the American and Australian intelligence agencies remained sceptical for several reasons, the foremost being that, if true, they would look considerably foolish for having allowed themselves to be duped by the Russian operation to place sleeper agents into the western fold. The fact that they couldn't find the last scientist did raise red flags; however, as the Greyfin team had previously considered, the scientists may have had some internal agreement in place that ensured once the first one went missing, then they all went to ground. If they were legitimate as first thought, then they would have had plenty to fear from a vengeful Russian government.

What was to say this wasn't all a big lie established by some Russian intelligence officer trying to get his brother out of the Ukraine? Kryton's new mission was to find out what the truth actually was. Until they could work out what was actually happening, he would take everything presented to him by the Israelis with a grain of salt.

He pressed the button on his green G-Shock watch to illuminate the time. The meeting should have started ten minutes ago. He leaned back on his SUV and looked up at the sky as he rubbed his hands.

He wasn't expecting to see anything – the UAV was far too high for the naked eye. A few moments later, the glow of approaching headlights came across the sandy berms, piercing through the still dark, early morning sky.

"Inbound to your location," came the voice of the UAV pilot across his earpiece.

"Acknowledged."

The lights came increasingly closer, until Kryton could make out the shape of an SUV – almost identical to his own except for the lighter colour – speeding towards him at such pace that it was kicking up sand off of the road. He stood up and took a pace forward, raising his hand across his eyes to block out the brightness of the headlights. The SUV stopped several metres in front of him, and the headlights suddenly dimmed.

Kryton was annoyed. He had allowed himself to be put on the backfoot by being blinded by the lights. However, there had been no signals or meeting tradecraft pre-arranged. It was a straight up meeting of two people in the middle of the night. He tilted his head away from the front of the other SUV to allow his peripheral vision to do the work whilst the front of his cornea recalibrated itself. The engine of the SUV remained running for a few moments. Kryton lowered his arm to expose his face, and looked through the driver's side windscreen. All he could see was the outline of a large person.

The engine was turned off, and the driver's side door opened. The lone figure got out and approached Kryton, stopping a few paces in front of him. Kryton widened his eyes as his vision returned to normal, and closely examined the figure in front of him. It was a familiar face, but one only to now he had seen either through grainy footage or at a distance in a Dubai pub.

Boyd.

Kryton took a few paces forward himself and looked the man up and down. The man mirrored the action, and the two lethal intelligence operators spent a few seconds sizing each other up. Few things intimidated Kryton, but he knew that the lightly bearded man standing in front of him, of equal size and build, would be a formidable opponent.

121

"Shall we?" asked Kryton, gesturing towards the small building that had once held Greyfin's two Mossad detainees.

Boyd paused for a moment, looking around before nodding and following Kryton inside. The two men entered and sat across from each other at a small wooden table inside the otherwise empty building, illuminated by several small lights dangling from the ceiling.

They sat in silence for a moment. Kryton started to get the feeling that this man wanted to be there even less than he did; perhaps another Mossad agent so committed to his work that he also had an intense distrust of outsiders. If so, then he was someone more alike to Kryton than he first thought. The Australian pulled a piece of A4 sized paper from his pocket and placed it on the table in front of the Israeli spy, before breaking the silence.

"Did the Mossad kill an Australian citizen by the name of Andrew Boyd?"

The man leaned in and looked down, seeing copies of the identification page of two passports – identical in almost every way save for the different photos. One of the images was of the actual Andrew Boyd, whilst the other was of the man now sitting in front of Kryton. He then leaned back and looked at the Australian.

"No, we didn't," he replied neutrally. "We utilise a third party that manages a morgue in the Middle East. They help facilitate the passports of dead western tourists for our use."

Kryton looked at the Israeli man, whose face betrayed no emotions. He was obviously well trained and experienced, and it appeared that he had been briefed to work with the Australian. Kryton knew that he was telling the truth, however, as the Greyfin investigation into the fate of the real Andrew Boyd had found that he had been killed in a bus crash about two years earlier. The question was asked simply to determine whether the Israelis were there genuinely or not.

"We've been looking for you. You hurt one of my people in Dubai. You also shot at Australian soldiers. You could have killed them," said Kryton.

The Israeli shook his head dismissively.

"If I wanted to kill them, they'd be dead," he said nonchalantly.

The lack of smugness or brashness in the reply only enhanced Kryton's belief that the assassin sitting in front of him was a competent professional. He looked across the table, still trying to size up his opponent. The eyes gave away plenty, and Kryton could tell that the man had seen and done plenty in the shadowy world in which they both served.

"We didn't know who you were in Dubai. We thought you could have been a Russian team looking to stop us, or even a terrorist group. We'll take our punishment for that. It's only fair," added the Israeli, in a rapid change of tone and demeanour.

The statement appeared sincere and given willingly, catching Kryton by surprise. It suggested to the Australian that it was as close to an apology that they would likely get. After a moment of silence, he stood up and walked around to the other side of the table. The Israeli stood up to meet the approaching Australian, who extended his hand peacefully.

"My name is Zach Kryton."

The Mossad officer looked at the offered hand for a moment, before reaching down and firmly reciprocating the gesture.

"My name is Uri Cohen. Mossad. We have reason to believe that something big is coming that will be a major threat."

"Threat? To whom?" asked Kryton cautiously.

The seasoned assassin rubbed his hand across his beard and looked at Kryton forebodingly.

"To all of us, Mister Kryton. To all of us."

Zach Kryton will be back in *Greyzone*

Please feel free to follow us on social media and
provide recommendations and feedback!

INSTAGRAM

joshfrancis_red.diamond

FACEBOOK

joshfrancisbooks

INSTAGRAM

FACEBOOK

AMAZON

Please leave an honest review on Amazon. This helps to tailor better
content and allows for reader interaction.

Sign up to the readers group

Biography

Josh Francis qualified as high school teacher before commissioning into the Royal Australian Navy as a junior officer soon after the September 11 attacks in the US. A desire to serve on warlike operations saw him resign his commission and enlist into the Australian Army. After qualifying as an infantryman and paratrooper, Josh deployed on peacekeeping operations in Timor-Leste conducting counter-militia operations.

After completing basic and specialist intelligence operations training, Josh completed multiple deployments to Afghanistan and Iraq, conducting duties in conventional and special operations, as well as training roles.

He is the author of the military themed personal development books *The Camouflage Series*, as well as the *Zach Kryton* series of books. His debut book is titled *Under the Pump*, a memoir about his youthful antics whilst working at a petrol station in his hometown of Adelaide.

www.ingramcontent.com/pod-product-compliance
Lightning Source LLC
Chambersburg PA
CBHW070341130626
46556CB00007B/2970